Mollie Mouse and Her Christmas Choir

Eva R. Priestley

2019

An Amazon Book

Mollie's Idea and how it Came About

"Teach me how to sing," said little Mollie and looked at her mother with pleading, pearly round eyes. "I want to join the Christmas choir."

Mama Mouse stared at her sweet baby and, at first, did not know what to think. She had never heard of a mouse having the wish to sing.

What are you talking about, dear child?" she finally asked. "Mice don't sing. And they don't have choirs."

"Why not? I heard people children sing when I ran through the church one day, and they sounded so very pretty. All those voices together … heavenly!"

"But, Mollie, how would you know what heavenly is?" Mama Mouse could not believe that her little girl was suddenly coming up with strange ideas. She shook her head in wonder.

"I heard the man in the white robe talk about a place called Heaven. And how beautiful it is there. And about angels singing on a certain night when a baby boy was born. He talked about Christmas."

"When was that, Mollie? When did you hear all this?"

"That day when you and Millie were in the church kitchen, looking for crumbs for us to eat, and our big, fat brother, Morris, even found a piece of cheese, which he didn't want to share until you made him."

"You should have stayed with us instead of sneaking around all by yourself."

Molly made a face as if she was sorry, but she really wasn't. Her experience had been too precious to have been missed. She couldn't get the lovely voices of the people children out of her head.

Mama Mouse Steps In

"How can I learn to sing?" Mollie asked again.

"I don't know the answer to this," Mama Mouse said, "but I have an idea worth trying. Open your mouth and make a loud squeak. Then try real hard to make it higher. I think you have to let the sound come out from closer to the top of your head."

Mollie tried it right away, and when Millie happened to come by, she got a laughing fit, because her sister's facial expression was so funny. Crunched up. Mouth wide open. Eyes almost closed. And the squeak was so unnaturally high that it sounded as if Mollie was in pain.

4

Mama Mouse had to suppress a giggle, but Mollie seemed proud of her accomplishment. Then Mama had an idea. "Mollie," she said, "don't close your eyes. Try it with your eyes wide open. Raise your eyelids. I think this will help."

Mollie did as told. Indeed, this trick improved the sound tremendously.

Mama Mouse applauded.

"Now I have to squeak lower."

Again, Mama thought hard. Finally, she said, "Try this. Make your squeak come out from down in your chest."

"Thank you. I will try." So Mollie made a face that looked very serious, and she forced her squeak to come out from way below. It sounded more like a growl than a squeak.

"Are we having company?" Morris asked as he burst through the mouse hole. He looked around, but he could not see a stranger who might own a gravelly voice.

"That's our Mollie practicing to sing pretty." Millie pointed to her sister.

"You call this pretty?" Morris asked. "I call it horrible."

Very much disappointed, Mollie stopped.

"Only practice makes perfect," Mama Mouse explained. "Don't make fun of your sister. She's trying to learn to sing. And, actually, I think we should all give it a try. I will, too. And … if we succeed, then we will tell all our friends and the neighbors about it and invite them to come over for singing lessons. By the time Christmas comes around, we will have a regular choir like the people."

"Yeah!" Mollie shouted and made a joyful little leap.

Morris, at first, scowled, but then he, too, agreed to practice.

"But, but …" he stuttered after a short while. "I don't think it's a good idea for me."

"Why not?" Mama Mouse wanted to know.

"Because all the others are going to make fun of me. None of the kids play with me, and that's why they wouldn't want to be with me in a choir."

"Nonsense!" Mama Mouse shouted.

"That's true, Mama," Millie said. "The other mice always make fun of Morris. They call him horrible names. It's called bullying."

"I never heard of anything like this." Mama Mouse shook her head. "Why would they bully our Morris?"

"Because he has lost part of his tail in an accident. And one of his ears has a piece missing."

"That's not his fault."

"We know it isn't," Millie said. And Mollie nodded in agreement.

"That's beyond my understanding." Mama Mouse looked saddened. But then, after a moment, she declared, "We'll go ahead with the idea anyway and see what happens. You kids start practicing … right away … and I will run through the neighborhood and spread the news."

"Yeah, yeah, yeah!" the three mouse children shouted and raced around in circles, because that's how happy they were.

Happiness in the Basement

"We're going to have a Christmas choir! We're going to have a Christmas choir!" they squeaked. And without realizing it, their voices already changed to different tone levels. It sounded like music.

All this gaiety took place in the basement, which was not used by the people too often. Youth groups had their meetings there, in the big room, and the janitor kept his supplies in a closet off to the side. All holiday decorations were stored there, too, and the mice often climbed from shelf to shelf in hopes of new discoveries. The colorful Christmas decorations fascinated them most.

Though they did not know what they meant, they enjoyed looking at them. They scampered over and around them, unless the pretty things were hidden in sealed boxes. Sometimes, they nibbled holes in the boxes. But when the holes were discovered, the mice could hear the people scream, "Set traps! Now! The church mice are here again!"

If women heard the news, they cried out, "Eek!" as if they were afraid of cute little grey mice.

"Silly people," Mama Mouse would say, but she always told her children to quickly disappear into the hole behind the counter until the coast was clear again. "And be absolutely quiet. Not a peep or squeak out of you."

Mollie, Millie and Morris always obeyed. No way did they want to be caught by the church people.

But on this day, on which they had begun their singing practice, it seemed safe to be in the basement, and they skittered around table and chair legs, and they even dared to climb up onto the old piano. The big thing was stored there, because someone had said it was out of tune and not worth fixing.

The merriment went on.

"We're singing, yeah, yeah, we're singing! And soon we're going to have a Christmas choir!"

Loudest of all was Morris. In fact, his voice had improved so much in the briefest time that Mollie declared he must be a born singer. Millie agreed wholeheartedly.

Mama's News

When Mama Mouse returned, she could hardly believe her ears. *Are these my children?* she wondered. *Is it possible, really possible, that they can sing?*

Though she was happy about her children's quick learning, she was also worried that their joyful noise could be heard by someone in the church. This would be dangerous. Very dangerous. So she hushed them immediately. This, of course, was a big disappointment for the young ones.

"Did you tell everyone about our idea?" Millie asked.

Without waiting for her mother's answer, Mollie also asked, "Did you, Mama? And what did they say?"

Mama Mouse's sad face told it all.

"I knew it!" Morris looked grim. "I knew it!" he repeated. "They all thought it was a silly idea, and, also, they don't want to come because of me." Then he turned and raced as fast as he could into the hole behind the counter.

Mollie and Millie huddled close to their mother. They felt the need to comfort each other.

"What did they really say?" Mollie asked.

"For one thing, they told me it was a dumb idea. Mice don't sing. And, as Morris guessed, the children don't want to be around your brother. So I told the mothers about the bullying that was going on. They claimed they didn't know about it. But they promised they would have a good talk with their children."

"What are we going to do now?" Mollie looked to her mother for an answer.

"We keep on practicing. Soon we will all have good voices. And, guess what? I heard that the entire mouse community is going to come together in a few days for a talent show. Some mice have been working on stunts they are going to perform. Judges will decide who can climb a pole fastest, who can make the loudest noise, and who can eat the most cheese in an allotted time. And, can you imagine? One youngster knows how to gnaw pictures into wood. Children, it's going to be a lot of fun."

"I know what we are going to do, Mama," Mollie said right away. "We are going to sing and win first prize."

"All right." Mama Mouse smiled and then gave three nods.

"Will you sing with us?" Mollie wanted to know.

Mama Mouse had to think about it for a moment. Then she said, "I better leave the singing to my three children. I will conduct."

"Good idea," her daughters declared in unison.

Though Morris needed some convincing, he agreed to continue his singing lessons and to appear in the talent show.

The Talent Show

All too quickly, the day arrived. Never before had a talent show been arranged, so this was something extra special in the lives of the local mouse population.

"Look at Alex climb the pole! He's really good."

"How much more cheese can Mick fit into his stomach? I hope he won't burst," whispered an old field mouse.

Then it was Marcie's turn to do her art work on a sliver of wood.

"She's amazing!" The crowd watched in awe.

"I guess she's going to win the first prize," someone said loud enough for all to hear.

A balancing act on a red Christmas ball was funny to watch. The small mouse youngster fell off repeatedly but always climbed on again for another try. Finally, the judges made him stop.

A big, fat mouse's screech was ear-piercing. Nobody seemed to appreciate it.

In general, some talents were too ordinary to reap much applause, others were quite remarkable.

Mama Mouse and her children were last on the list. It was evident that the onlookers did not expect much of the group of singers. But they were in for a big surprise. As soon as the first notes could be heard, a hush fell over the audience.

Singing mice. A novelty. Beautiful. And the boy's voice – how strong, how clear! Suddenly, all fell in love with Morris. He was the darling of the crowd, and this signaled the end of all bullying.

"And the first prize goes … to the singing church mice," the lead judge declared.

Mama Mouse pushed Mollie to receive the Blue Ribbon, for singing had been her idea.

Hesitating, Mollie took a few steps forward. Then she stopped and turned to the row of judges. After a few long moments of just staring from one to the other, she said to them, "I cannot accept the award all by myself. There are three of us, Morris, Millie and I. We were all singing. And our mama directed us. Directing is an important job, too. She even taught us how to sing. Wouldn't you say it's only fair that we all come forward to get our ribbon?"

"Yes, let them all come forward to receive the honor!" the crowd roared. "Honors to the four church mice!"

The three judges seemed perplexed. But as the roar grew louder, one of them stood up, lifted one paw and shouted, "Silence! I hear you. I agree with Mollie.

Will the entire singing group please step up to receive the ribbon?"

And that's exactly what happened. Mama Mouse and her three children were honored together.

Everybody Wants to Sing

As soon as the talent show was officially over, whole families of mice ringed Mama Mouse and her children. All had the same questions. "Can you teach us to sing?" "May we join your choir?" "When would you like us to come over?"

"Hold on a minute," Mama Mouse interrupted the clamor. "Not all at once, please. We have to take one question at a time."

She waited until everyone was quiet, took a deep breath, looked over the assembly of friends and neighbors, and then said, "It is my belief that you can do anything you set your mind to. It needs the will to succeed and practice,

practice, practice. As we have shown you today, mice can sing. And singing brings happiness. You are happy with your new-found talent, and you make other people happy when they listen to your voices. But I see that there are so many of you. I cannot handle such a large number all by myself. Perhaps my children will be willing to help. We could have separate groups first, and then, later, we can put them together. Just imagine, one big choir! But we have a problem."

Before she had a chance to explain the problem, lots of anxious looks came her way. She saw great disappointment in the faces of her admirers. "What is the problem?" they asked. "You didn't mention a problem before. You were eager for us to join."

"That was before I knew how many of you wanted to sing." Mama Mouse needed a moment to think how to best explain the situation. Then, with a big sigh, she said, "We cannot have so many mice in the building. The church people would notice, and then they kill us for sure. You all know how they do it. With traps. With poison. They even hit us with big brooms until we are dead. For that reason, we have to find a safer place."

"Oh, my! And our hole in the field isn't big enough," moaned one mouse.

"We live in a barn," said one. "But there's a cat. Cats eat mice. We always have to be very careful that this cat doesn't get us. The barn is not a safe place to meet."

The prospects looked slim. Mama Mouse hung her head low, and so did the other mice. Some were ready to leave the meeting.

A Happy Turn of Events

Even Mama Mouse thought it best to take her children home. How terribly disappointed they would be when she told them the news.

But then, suddenly, a youngster came running to the front. "I've got it! I've got it!" he was shouting.

All eyes turned to the boy. It was Jake, the one who had kept falling off the pretty Christmas ball. When they recognized who it was, the grown-up mice began to laugh. Poor Jake had a reputation of not being the smartest little mouse fellow, but everybody liked him nonetheless.

"What have you got, little boy?" the old field mouse asked.

"I know of a good place to practice."

"And where might this be?" the field mouse's younger companion asked with a broad grin.

"In the woodshed."

"Which woodshed?"

"There's one on the other side of the field. Nobody goes there anymore. I mean no people. We little field mice are there all the time. It's the best place to play. We love to climb up and down the stacks of wood. There are so many places to play hide and seek. No cats, no dogs, no people, just mice … and spiders."

"How far away is this woodshed from here? Not too far, I hope, because, you see, I can't travel that far anymore. My old legs are getting tired."

"I know where it is," said the companion of the old mouse who had just voiced her concern. "In fact, the shed Jake is talking about is right near where you live."

"Really?"

"Yes, you only forgot, because you don't get out much anymore."

"I can't learn to sing at my age, but I would like to listen. It would give me much pleasure."

Mama Mouse was happy the way things were turning out. She set a time when they would meet, and since the old woodshed was supposedly large enough to accommodate all, everyone could rehearse at the same time, but in different corners.

While most mice were still gathered closely around Mama Mouse, not only discussing the upcoming rehearsals but also exchanging family news and the prospect of a long, harsh winter, a group of youngsters amused itself off to the side.

Mollie and Millie were the most popular, mainly with the girl mice, but some of the boys also paid them special attention. A few even started to flirt with them. Alex was the most eager to vie for Mollie's favor.

"Mollie," he said, "you can sing high, but I can climb high. Would you like me to show it to you again?"

Not really interested, but not wanting to make Alex feel bad, she said, "Okay. Let's see how fast you can limb all the way up to the top."

It was a very high pole, and even for the talent show, Alex had not made it completely to the top. But now he was determined to do it. Yes, he would get to the top, even if it took the last ounce of his strength.

"Ha, he can't do it. It's much too high," said one of the older mouse girls. "Alex is a big showoff. Don't fall for his trick, Mollie."

Mollie didn't answer. She knew Priscilla was jealous. Most likely, she had an eye on Alex and was upset that he paid attention to her, Mollie.

"Perhaps you can catch me a star while you are up there," she said to the climber. "The first ones are just coming out. Catch me the star that stood over Bethlehem."

"What are you talking about?" Millie asked, and the other mice chimed in with their questions. "What is this silly babble? The star of Bethlehem. Are you making up stories again? First you sing, something no mouse has done before, and now you are talking about a strange star. Indeed, what is it with you, Mollie?"

This was not the reaction Mollie had expected. Why did all those ignorant mouse youngsters make fun of her? Even Millie, her own sister. And Morris. Why didn't her brother, at least, come to her defense? *Where is he, anyhow?* she thought. *I haven't seen him for quite some time. He didn't sneak home by any chance?*

Her thoughts were interrupted when Millie spoke up. "You better explain about that star of Bethlehem. Did you make it up? Like a joke?"

"No, no, it's not a joke. I didn't make it up. I heard about it when I hid in a corner of the church while the people man in the white robe talked about Christmas. There was a bright star over a place called Bethlehem. And a baby was born. A very special baby. And at Christmas, people celebrate this baby's birth. And remember, I heard the people choir rehearse for this Christmas Day. Their voices were so beautiful that I wanted to sing, too. And you know the rest."

"Oh, I wish I could've listened to that story and heard the people sing!" Marcie gave a big sigh.

"Then I invite you to come for a sleepover to our hole in the church, and we can both sneak upstairs to where all the people sit on very long benches and listen to the man in white. But you have to be really quiet. Nobody is allowed to notice us."

Marcie promised.

In the meantime, Alex, by the pole, was getting impatient. "Do you want me to climb all the way up to the very top or not?" he asked.

"Okay, go ahead and climb!" Mollie shouted.

Run, Mice, Run!

All eyes were turned on Alex, who was obviously relieved that it was finally his turn to show off by attempting to reach the top of the pole. It wasn't just an ordinary pole. On it, fairly high up, it had a pretty decoration attached to it. People called this a Christmas wreath. Alex had in mind to make a brief stop there, sit on that wreath for a moment and dangle his hind legs. Or, perhaps, amble around the circular ornament, all the way around, and then, from there, go to the tip of the pole. Would he be able to hear applause from way up high?

Before starting out, he winked a few times at Mollie. He had to make sure she gave him her full attention.

A tiny starting jump, and Alex was on his way. At first, he made excellent progress. Then, getting a bit tired, he inched upward slower … and slower.

"You can do it, Alex!" the mouse kids cheered him on.

Pant, pant. A little higher he climbed. Off and on, he had to stop to catch his breath. His tiny paws hurt.

"Why don't you give up and just slide down?" some big boy mouse called up to the struggling Alex.

No, he wouldn't give up, and so he inched higher.

The wreath was in sight. Finally. It gave him hope. *Once I get up there,* he thought, *it gives me a good reason to rest.*

Right front paw up, left front paw up. Pull up the right leg, then the left, inch by inch … almost … there. And then, just as he believed he could get hold of a piece of the outer edge of that wreath, oh, no! Alex lost his footing and … slid back about three inches. It could have been worse, much worse. Still, tears began to flow.

"Brave mice don't cry," he chided himself. "Don't act like a baby." And after a series of deep sighs, he forced himself to continue his climb.

This time, when Alex was up to the wreath, he was extra careful. He had to make sure he would grasp a strong piece of whatever it was sticking out, and it had to be shaped just right for him to get hold of and hang on to. There! He reached for it, got a good grip, swung himself up onto the big round Christmas ornament, found a place to put his tiny behind, and indeed, he was finally in a safe position. He then lay down, flat, all the way. It was a wonderfully relaxing position.

"Oh, this feels good," he said to himself over and over again.

Triumphantly, he wildly waved to his friends on the ground. But since he was so high up, they only saw him as a tiny dot.

Alex enjoyed the view. In the very beginning, looking down had made him slightly dizzy, but this sensation had not lasted long. Just as he began to feel comfortable, daylight was fading. The world below became hidden under a grey veil. Then a few lights pierced though this veil, lights from houses. Street lights, too. And above, the stars appeared. Could one be the star of Bethlehem Mollie had talked about? But the longer he thought about it, the less likely it seemed. Supposedly, this bright star had appeared an eternity ago and for a special reason.

"I'm very confused about the whole thing," he mumbled to himself as he lay down again. "That's something people believe in, Mollie had said. It has no meaning for mice. Or does it?"

Before Alex got out of his relaxing position, his ears picked up familiar sounds. Dogs yapping. He lifted his head, then fixed his eyes on the ground below. Aha! The farmer had opened the barn door, and now bright light came streaming out. Not only light but also his three dogs. And, oh my, the cats were on the loose, too. Alex was well familiar with those cats, a whole bunch of them, and they were always hungry for mice. When on his own territory, he had to run into hiding as fast as he could, but while on the pole, he was safe from danger. At least from the danger of cats.

But, but, what about all my friends assembled down there? he thought and shuddered. *Cats have keen senses of smell. And so many mice together must give off an extra strong odor. In no time at all those bad cats will have my friends sniffed out, and then it's going to be the end of Mollie and Millie and … and … and so many others. What can I do?*

So Alex took a deep, deep breath, and then he let out the loudest squeaks and squeals he could manage. "Run, mice, run!" it meant, and because a friendly wind arrived at just the correct moment, Alex's warning was carried down to the ears of the other mice.

"Run, run, run!" The warning was repeated everywhere, and the mice took off in all directions, each determined to make it into a safe hole. By the time the cats arrived, all mice were underground. Only Alex was still up on his lofty pole. That's where he remained until cats and dogs were back in the barn again.

Alex looked up to the stars once more. He liked the way they were blinking. One star in particular gave off an extra bright light. *Could this, perhaps, be the star of Bethlehem?* he thought. Then he slid down the pole and, finding himself all alone, made his way to the place where his family lived. He felt mighty proud of himself for having saved his friends from the cats' attack.

Safely Home

The mouse youngsters, who had been by the pole, watching Alex, heard the warning first. Oh, how scared they were! How fast they ran to the cluster of grownups, screaming, "Cats on the way! Great danger! Out of here! Quickly, quickly! Mama, Papa, run!"

In no time at all, the gathering area was clear of mice. Left behind were only a few crumbs of cheese from the eating contest, and the pretty Christmas ball ornament.

"That was some scare," Mama Mouse said, quite out of breath, before she collapsed almost immediately after having squeezed through the narrow entrance to the hole where she and her family lived. At the moment, they were only four, she and her three children. Papa Mouse just happened to be out of town. He was seeing his ailing sister in a nearby town, where she had a rather safe hiding place in the house of a rich people family.

"Lie there and relax for a bit," Millie said and gave her mama a gentle pat. "Be thankful that we are all safe."

Mama Mouse nodded. Then she whispered, "I am so proud of you. I mean all three of you."

"And we are proud of you," Millie and Mollie said. "You taught us well. You even got the whole mouse population excited about singing. It was you who convinced them it can be done."

Morris, who stood slightly to the side, cleared his throat. This was his usual sign that he wanted to say something important.

"What is it?" Mama Mouse asked.

"Something really great happened. After we were done singing and had even won the Blue Ribbon, not a single kid made fun of me anymore. Suddenly, everybody liked me. It's a miracle. And I heard many say that, when the singers get split up into groups for the lessons, they want me as their teacher."

"You certainly made an impression," Mama Mouse said and, apparently recovered enough, stood back up on her four legs.

"But, children, let's not waste more precious time now. We have to sneak into the kitchen and find us some food. You know it has to be best done at night when no humans are around. So, let's go!"

"In all this excitement, I even forgot how hungry I was." Mollie giggled, and Millie joined in.

So, off to the kitchen they were. But, as they wanted to exit their hole, they found it blocked.

"Now what?" Mama said and pushed Morris out of the way. "Perhaps it's something easy to move. If not, then …"

"What then?" all the kids cried in unison.

"We'll have to use our teeth and gnaw a new hole."

Morris, Mollie and Millie stared at their mother as if she had suggested something impossible.

"Don't look at me like this," Mama Mouse said sternly. "Remember, if you really set your mind to something, you can do it. Think of your singing."

Morris grumbled something.

"What did you say?" Mama Mouse asked. "I couldn't understand a single word." She gave him a disapproving look.

"Learning to sing is fun, but gnawing a new hole is work."

Hearing this, Mama shook her head. *My boy has a lot of growing up to do,* she thought. And for that reason, she ordered him to go ahead and try to push whatever was blocking the hole out of the way.

Morris, realizing he better do as told, prepared himself for a great impact with the obstructing object. *Ouch, ouch,* went through his mind even before he got there.

"One, two, three … now!" he said, rammed … what was it? Something so light that it slid out of the way and caused Morris to glide right out of the hole and into the church kitchen, where he came, with a bump, to a quick stop at the back of the counter.

Somewhat dazed, he looked around, slowly, to determine what in the world had just happened. What was this thing that had blocked the exit but could be pushed away so easily? A pouch of some sort. From the top of it, something shiny was sticking out. It needed to be investigated.

Just as Morris was creeping toward the strange pouch, he heard a familiar voice coming from behind him.

"Morris! Curiosity has killed many a mouse."

Could it be? Yes, it was. Papa Mouse had returned, and he was hugging something that looked really heavy, wrapped up in colorful paper. It was the kind of paper Morris had seen the humans use this time of year.

"Papa, Papa, you have come home!" Morris cried out. "We've been waiting for you. And we have so much to tell you."

Surprises for Everyone

Mama Mouse and her daughters stood with their eyes and mouths wide open. Never had they seen Morris go so fast. And how he had unclogged the doorway with such ease! Amazing, simply amazing! And then they heard the familiar voices, Morris's first and then … could it be? … Papa's deep one. What a wonderful surprise! Forgotten was the idea of finding that food in the kitchen. Celebrating dear Papa Mouse's return was much more important.

So they all scrambled out of the hole and formed a ring around their papa. They shouted happy welcomes and tried to report the good news, but he silenced them. "Please, please, not all at once. I cannot understand a word. It's a jumble. Kids, listen, let your mother speak first. Please."

"We missed you so much, dear." Mama Mouse lovingly rubbed her left shoulder against her husband's. "Come on in. But what is it you are carrying? I hope it fits through our opening."

"What did you bring, Papa?" Mollie wanted to know after also having given her father a loving rub.

Millie, too, was eager to find out what was under the pretty wrapping, but first she gave her father a warm welcome.

"And there's more." Morris jumped aside and pointed to the pouch he had so easily pushed out of the way.

"Kids, bring the light bundle in. You can handle it," Papa Mouse ordered. "It's full of surprises."

"I'll do it!" they shouted in unison, and in their eagerness to help, almost ripped the pouch to pieces.

"What did you bring us?" Now it was Millie who asked that question.

"You will see, my curious child. But first let's bring everything into our cozy hole where it's safer than out here."

"Yes, Papa," the two girls answered.

Then Papa Mouse turned to his son and said, "You can help me push the big bag through the hole."

"Okay." Morris was ready to do his part. But no matter how hard father and son shoved, the fat bag would not fit through the opening.

"It's no use," Papa Mouse finally declared. "We'll have to think of another way to bring the goodies in."

So he thought very hard, and then he had an idea. "Aha! Why didn't I think of it right away? We'll take something out, and the girls can carry it in, piece by piece, and when the bag isn't quite so full, you and I will be able to push it through the hole."

Oh, what wonderful things came out of the bag! Presents from the place Papa had visited, from the rich folks in whose house Papa's sister lived.

Mama Mouse had to scoot out of the way. She was just as excited as her children.

How did he lug those bundles here? He could not have done it by himself, she thought. *Someone, I'm sure, must have helped him.*

Moments later, she found out. It was her brother-in-law who had come along. And behind him appeared little Emmie, her daughters' favorite cousin.

"We thought we would surprise you," said Uncle Mouse. "We haven't seen each other for quite some time, and my Emmie missed her cousins."

"You have come just at the right time," Mollie declared with a mysterious smile.

"The right time for what?" Emmie asked. "Is it something good that's going on?"

"Even I am curious," Papa Mouse chimed in. "You were eager to tell me something before, but I wouldn't let you, because we had to bring in the bundles first. But now I think hearing the news is more interesting than showing you what presents I have brought for all of you. So, who wants to go first?"

"Let me! Let me! Let me!" his three children shouted at once, and Mama Mouse looked as if she was as eager as the young ones. Then she said, "I believe we should let Mollie tell you what's going on. It had been her idea that made it happen."

After a short hesitation, Mollie began, "We have learned to sing, and we are going to form a Christmas choir."

"You are joking, right?" Emmie started to giggle. "Ha, ha, mice don't sing! Never heard of it."

"This I want to hear." Papa Mouse also sounded amused, and he gave his wife a quizzical look.

"It's true, dear."

"I'm speechless."

"Then listen to them."

"Okay, let's hear it. Mollie, Millie, Morris, I'm all ears."

"Mama, will you direct us?" Mollie asked.

"Sure. Why not?"

How quickly they came together, watched for Mama Mouse's cue, and then, without a single miss of a note, performed like at the talent show.

Papa Mouse was stunned. It took him a few moments to find his voice. And Emmie, totally delighted, kept saying, "I want to sing, too. I want to sing, too. Teach me how to do it."

"Not now." Morris was getting impatient. His stomach cried for food. "I'm hungry. We were on our way to find crumbs in the kitchen when all this happened. This big delay! Can't we talk later?" He was ready to bolt out of the hole, but Papa Mouse blocked his way.

"Tonight, neither you nor anyone else here is going to forage for food." Then he pointed to the big bag and told Morris to dig out what was in it, and he told the girls to open the small bags that had already been taken out to slim down the big, fat one so it could fit through the entrance.

Oh, what wonderful surprises came out of the bags! Cheeses, such nice, big chunks. Pieces of crumbly cake. Bread crusts. Morsels of cereal, the yummy, sweetened kind. And … chocolates, every mouse's delight. Wow! There was enough for seven very hungry mice and some left over.

When the feasting was done, the events of the previous days were told, and Mollie showed the Blue Ribbon.

"What's the raggedy piece of ribbon for?" Emmie asked and wrinkled her tiny nose. "I guess some people kid lost it or threw it away, because it looks so old."

"That, that," Mollie stuttered, "is our precious ribbon for winning first place in the talent show."

"And we are mighty proud of it," declared Millie, giving her cousin a look that was way from friendly.

"When you see what's in the small pouch, then you won't think so highly of your piece of faded string."

"Emmie, be nice," warned Mama Mouse. "You always have to remember that our family does not live in a rich house, and we have learned to treasure the simple things, especially when they are earned."

"We practiced hard. Singing does not come easy. And if you want to learn it, too, then you have to put all your heart and soul into it." Morris hadn't looked so serious in a long time. "Okay, Emmie, do you still think you want to take our lessons? Actually, Mama is the best teacher. We learned from her."

Emmie thought it over for a minute or two, and she creased her little forehead so that it gave her cousins a laughing fit. But then, still a little hesitant, she said, "Yes, I will give it a try. When can we start?"

"Not after we have shown what's in the small pouch."

"I almost forgot about that one." Emmie giggled. Then she brought the lightweight bundle to the center of the mouse room, ripped the cover off, and, voila, out tumbled all kinds of shiny and colorful things. There was some tinsel, something people families decorated their trees with, those needle trees they brought into their homes this time of year, and there were some tiny, pretty ornaments – even a shiny glass ball similar to the one that had been used in the talent show, and colorful pieces of ribbon in better shape than the Blue Ribbon given out as first prize.

And there was something very special for Mama Mouse. A scarf. She had never owned a scarf before, and when Papa Mouse spread it over her head, she wished she could take a look at herself. But, of course, no mirror was in her home. Going upstairs, where she knew one was located, would have been too risky. So she had to rely on the judgment of her family. Everybody told her she looked very pretty, especially her husband. This made her feel very, very happy, and she began to sing.

Soon, the children joined in, even Papa Mouse – his voice was very deep, and Emmie produced a few really high squeaks.

The merriment went on until morning was about to break, and, all tired out, six mice went to sleep, but Uncle Mouse sneaked out to go back home.

Emmie Is Eager

"Squeak, squeak, squeak." Painful sounds woke up the mouse family way before their usual time to start the day.

"You there … quiet, please!" Papa Mouse shouted. "We had a rough night, all of us, and we need more sleep."

Emmie, who had been restless for some time already, because she had not been able to get the prospect of learning to sing out of her mind, was more than eager to begin the new day. Now Uncle Mouse was cross with her, and this made her sad. "Sorry," she whispered. "I'm so sorry."

Still in a state of half sleep, Morris, too, had overheard the very strange

51

squeaking. At first, he was thinking he was dreaming, perhaps, but then he remembered that his father was back home, and he had brought along little Emmie. Actually, Emmie wasn't quite so little anymore. She had grown since their last meeting, but she was about two weeks younger than he and his sisters, so this qualified her to be called little. But why was she making such painful noises when she should be asleep? "What's wrong with you?" he asked.

"I'm trying to sing."

"Don't try it before we teach you how to go about it. Otherwise, I'm sure – at least I think I'm sure – you may hurt your voice and sound horrible for the rest of your life. And then you may never find a husband. You don't want to ruin your chances, do you?"

"Oh, no, this can't happen." Emmie looked miserable, as if she was ready to cry.

"I have an idea," Morris whispered to his cousin. "Let's sneak over to the very far end of our tunnel. There is a small bend, and when we are around that corner and practice there, I'm sure the others will not hear us. They can sleep undisturbed while we squeeze in our first lesson. Agreed?"

Emmie eagerly nodded.

And so the two pitter pattered, as quietly as possible, to that corner at the very end of the tunnel.

Morris remembered every word his mother had told him and his sisters about how to reach the high notes and then how to produce the low ones.

First, he made Emmie try the high squeaks. The first ones came out so badly that he was tempted to give up. *I fear she's unteachable,* he thought. But then, all of a sudden, the sounds she made became clearer.

"Yes, yes, Emmie, I think you've got it!"

She stopped and looked at him in surprise.

"Don't stop!" he shouted. "Keep on practicing. Practice makes perfect. That's what Mama said."

When Morris was satisfied with Emmie's high notes, he told her how to reach the low notes.

Her first grunts were horrible. So horrible that she scared herself.

"Loosen up a bit," Morris advised.

She did. It worked.

"Now we are going to mix the high notes with the low notes to make a nice melody. I do it first, and then you imitate me."

It did not take long, and Emmie did so well that Morris dared to suggest they sing together.

"Wow, you are remarkable, Emmie! Wait until we demonstrate it to the others."

Happily singing, the two returned to the place where the rest of the family was already waking up.

"Where have you been?" Mama Mouse asked as soon as she saw them coming. "And what have you been up to? I hope you didn't get into any mischief."

"Mischief?" the two asked, looking at each other and then to Mama Mouse. "No mischief. We've been working."

"Working? Doing what?" Now Papa Mouse wanted answers.

"Morris taught me to sing," Emmie said with laughter in her voice. "He has been a wonderful teacher."

"Oh, my," was all Papa Mouse was able to say to that, and Mama Mouse displayed a satisfied smile.

Mollie and Millie performed a joyful dance, with Morris and Emmie joining in. And while they were dancing, they made up a happy tune.

"Come on, Mama and Papa, sing and dance with us. Soon we will be known as The Singing Mouse Family and become famous," said Mollie, "but first I want to have my Christmas choir."

Off to the Woodshed?

At last it was time to set out for the woodshed, the agreed upon place where singing lessons were to be held. The shed was located way out in the field, and Papa Mouse, who had made the big trek from his sister's house the day before, was not eager to be on the road again. But when he explained this to his family, they did not want to hear excuses from him.

"Papa, you have to come with us," Mollie insisted. "At least you have to try to make some pleasant noises. It may be difficult at first, but with practice, I'm sure, even you can learn to sing. The lower notes, perhaps. They are needed. In the people choir, the men sing them. The director called them the basses."

"You didn't tell us about basses before," Millie said and looked at her sister accusingly.

"So what. Nobody asked. Perhaps you should have come to listen yourself to what is going on upstairs."

"I'm too afraid to go there."

"Well, that's your fault."

"Children, children, really, you need to behave yourselves," Mama Mouse interrupted the quarrel. "We have to get on our way. Are you ready? And you," she pointed at Papa Mouse, "you better come along. As Mollie said, deep voices are needed, too."

"What do I sing?" Morris wanted to know. "I'm not singing all the way down there like what you call the basses, but I'm also not singing as high as you girls. Did you maybe learn a name for this, too, Mollie?"

"Yes. You are in the tenor range. Millie, Emmie and I are sopranos. Mama, who is a little lower, is an alto."

"Oh, my goodness, what a smart little daughter I have!" Mama Mouse exclaimed. "But now, honestly, let's go."

And so they all slipped out of the hole, darted through the kitchen and were about to make their way upstairs to sneak outdoors through their secret exit, when they heard footsteps, loud, heavy human footsteps.

Whoever was coming down was not allowed to see them. No! It would mean disaster for them. Deadly mousetraps everywhere. Morris had once made the acquaintance with one of those nasty traps meant for killing. He had been lucky. Only his tail got caught. It still made him shudder when he thought of it. He had struggled hard, trying to free himself. Papa Mouse had come to his rescue. He pulled him by the ear. Ouch! In the process, a bit of Morris's ear got ripped off, and when the terrified boy finally came loose, the trap kept part of his tail. Healing took some time, but he was alive.

Then the taunting began. Indeed, his former friends were bullying him. Until the talent show. And now, just when singing lessons for all interested were going to start, Morris and his family had to run for their lives again.

Hide, hide! Back into the hole! Wait until the footsteps disappear, was on everyone's mind.

When the last mouse had slipped through the hole, Papa counted heads. Alarmed, he shouted, "Only five! One is missing."

"Oh, dear," Mama Mouse exclaimed, shaking her head, "you forgot to count yourself."

Now!

Inside their safe home, the church mice listened. They heard people footsteps coming and going, some voices and happy laughter, too, but then there was quiet. Still, they waited a while longer to make sure no people would return. Then they made their way out of the hole, very carefully.

Halfway into the kitchen, by the table, they stumbled onto something very enticing. Food. Lots of food.

"That's what they did here," Papa Mouse said. "They had a feast. Lucky for us. They left crumbs. Look at all those crumbs!"

"Now we can have a feast, too." Morris performed a dance. That's how happy he was. Immediately, he started to stuff himself.

Mollie, Millie and Emmie daintily picked up a few crumbs here and there.

"Children," Mama Mouse warned, "don't waste more time. We are late already. When we return, you may have your fill."

"But what if some people person comes to sweep everything away while we are gone?" Emmie asked.

"Yeah, it may happen," Morris groused. "And then we are out of luck. All this delicious food wasted."

"Stop it, Morris," Mama Mouse chided her son. "They never clean up well. They always leave some in the cracks and in the corners. Duty calls. We have to hurry to the woodshed."

The one most reluctant to leave was Papa Mouse. First of all, he was not too happy that his family made him go to rehearsal, and then, of course, he would have loved to stay where so much good food was there for the taking. But Mama gave him a good, hard shove, and so he followed the others out of the church, across a large parking lot that was just beginning to ice up a little, then over a cold field, until they finally arrived at the woodshed.

"That was a long walk, and through all those dead blades and stiff stalks of whatever it used to be," moaned Emmie. "I'm not accustomed to this."

Mollie and Millie laughed at their cousin, who had no idea about country living.

"We walked across a field," Millie explained. "In the warm summer, everything is soft and green and good smelling. But then comes the ugly cold season. The grass loses its pretty color and turns dry, and so do the bigger stalks that used to have pretty flowers on top."

"If you say so." Emmie didn't seem very interested. But then, moments later, she thought an explanation was needed. "I know about flowers and grass. Where I live, they are in neat order, in gardens. In small gardens. My mama doesn't want me to go out there.

Neighborhood cats might get me, she tells me."

"After the talent show, we had to run away from cats," Molly said. "It was so scary."

"I bet it was," Emmie replied and moved faster.

Finally at the Woodshed

When the mouse family arrived at the woodshed, it received a mixed welcome.

"Where have you been? We waited and waited and almost gave up."

"We were afraid you might have changed your mind."

"Did you get lost?"

"Did you forget?"

"I think, it was quite inconsiderate of you to keep us waiting."

The remarks and questions came from all sides, and with so much babble going on at the same time, half of what was said could not be understood.

"Hold it! Hold it!" Mama Mouse squeaked in her loudest voice. "I'm sorry we are late, but it could not be helped.

We had to run back into our hole and wait until the humans cleared out. You can imagine what would have happened had they seen us."

"But, you see, now we are here," Morris chimed in, "and I guess we can get started."

"How do we begin?" one bright-eyed youngster asked.

"I'm really curious," the boy's father remarked. "Never, ever, would I have thought I might try to sing."

"Learning something new is always good, dear." His wife gave him a loving bump.

Mollie stepped forward, waited until all jabbering had stopped, and then she announced her plan. "This is how we should go about it. Mama will explain to you the basics. She did it for us, and it worked. So, pay very close attention, please."

All eyes turned to Mama Mouse.

She climbed onto a block of wood to be seen by all. Then she fixed her eyes on the listeners and began. "Tighten

your throats and think high. Force out
the air to squeak melodiously. It takes
some effort, but it works. Do it again.
And again. Try hard. Harder. With
practice, it will come easier. And when
you don't think quite as high, you will
produce a bit lower sound. Eventually,
you will be able to control it to form a
real melody, which, of course, we will all
do together. And the low notes, you will
have to form them deep down in your
chest."

Soon, all kinds of funny squeaks
could be heard. They were practice
squeaks. Some got clearer quicker than
others, depending on the abilities of the
participants.

Mollie mingled to listen to the
progress. She praised where praise was
deserved, and she gave hints where
help was needed. Millie and Morris did
the same, but Emmie remained in a
corner and practiced on her own.

After having closely listened to the
many individual voices, Mama Mouse
separated the mice into four groups. "Go

over there to my Mollie, Millie and little Emmie," she directed some. "And you and you and you, join my husband." "Hey, young fellows, can you see where Morris is? Go to him." "Stay with me," she told others.

And when Mama Mouse went through the crowd to separate the high voices from the low, she got many puzzled looks, because no one could figure out what this was all about.

"I have to give credit to Mollie," she finally explained. "Mollie learned, by watching the people choir, that there are four groups of voices, and all are equally important in a choir. The highest voices belong to the sopranos. They stand there in the corner with my girls. Then come the lower female voices, and they are the altos. That's this group here with me. All those over there with Morris are the tenors, the higher male voices. And the basses, those with the deep voices, are grouped around my husband. Now it is possible that, after you have all done a lot of practicing, it is discovered that your voice comes out lower or higher than expected right now. If this happens, you will be switched into a more suitable group before the serious rehearsals begin. But right now, go home and don't forget to practice, practice, practice. Only practice makes perfect."

"When will we meet again?" several mice asked.

"Can we do it again tomorrow?" a few others pleaded.

So they took a vote, and it was decided that they would wait two days to give everybody enough time to practice at home.

On the way out, Papa Mouse stopped for a moment to listen to what some of the young mice told each other. "I had hoped to be grouped with Mollie and Millie, but I was put somewhere else. Why do I have to sing with the males?" "And I wanted to be with Morris. But no, only boys and some daddies made it into his corner."

Papa Mouse felt like laughing, but he kept it in. And he didn't tell his children that he realized that some young mice of the opposite sex had crushes on them. Later, he mentioned it to his wife. She smiled broadly and rubbed her cheek against his, which meant "I love you."

The Sleepover

They were only a short distance from the gathering place, when they heard someone calling, "Mollie, Millie, wait up! I want to come with you. You said I could visit to hear the people choir and listen to the man in white. May I? Now?"

The caller was Marcie, and she was hurrying to catch up with her friends.

"But Marcie, did you ask your mother? Did she give you permission?" Mama Mouse asked the breathless youngster.

"Yes, I did. And she did give me permission."

"Okay then, join us. But you must not forget to be really quiet when we get into the church where we live. Don't ever let anybody see or hear you."

"I know, I know. Mollie warned me. No people person is allowed to notice us."

"A sleepover," Morris mumbled. "Now I have to put up with four girls. Four!"

"And what is so bad about this?" Mollie wanted to know.

Morris shrugged and refused to answer.

"Of course, you, dear brother, could join us when we go to listen. You, too, might find it interesting." Mollie grinned.

"We'll see. But first let's get home and see what's left on the kitchen floor. I'm starved."

"And I agree with you, Morris," Papa Mouse said. "My poor stomach is kind of rumbling, too."

"Oh, you guys, always thinking of food." Mama Mouse shook her head. But as soon as they reached the church and then had safely made their way downstairs and into the kitchen, she was as eager as Morris and her husband to fill her belly with the delicious crumbs the people had not bothered to sweep up from the floor. Of course, the four girls needed no urging to partake in the feast.

Later, they all discussed what a delightful evening they have had. Lots of friends at the meeting. Singing lessons. Food. And a great event ahead. They would be listening to the people choir and the man in white who talked about a baby boy having been born.

Suddenly, Mollie grew thoughtful. When Mama Mouse noticed her child's silence, she asked, "What's the matter, Mollie? Is something wrong? Has someone said or done something to upset you?"

"No, Mama, it isn't anything like that. It's … you know … we were all having so much fun that we forgot what we have to do. We have to practice singing. Papa and Marcie are completely new at it. Emmie only knows a little, and the rest of us are not perfect. We still have to learn to sing better. Having won the Blue Ribbon at the talent show doesn't mean we are ready for a great public performance. We still have to practice, practice, and practice more. That's what you told us in the beginning. Don't you remember?"

"You are right, my dear child. I hope our friends and neighbors, who have joined the group, are as serious about it as you."

"Let's split up. Millie and I will take on Emmie and Marcie. And you, Mama, you should try your luck with Papa, but at the end of the tunnel, away from us girls. Take Morris with you. Will that be okay?"

"I think it's a splendid idea. Wish me luck."

Papa Mouse had overheard the conversation. At first, he was not too happy about what was in store for him, and he had in mind to think of a good excuse to get out of this music lesson. He could feign a bad cold coming on, a nasty irritation of his throat. Or he could fake a series of yawn and claim to be much, much too tired to stay awake another minute. This, of course, would be rather unusual for a mouse, because the most active time for mice is at night. Being so very tired at this hour would indicate serious illness and probably cause worry to his whole family. No, he couldn't do this to his loved ones. And so he obediently followed his wife and son and even forced himself to look somewhat exited.

As soon as the three were in their designated spot in the tunnel, Mama Mouse asked her husband, "Do you remember what I taught everybody at the meeting? How do you produce the high notes?"

"You think high and force them out from way back in your throat. Oh, oh, excuse me, I mean high up. I tried it, and I could feel it in my ears. In fact, it gave me a headache."

"You are obviously not meant to be a soprano. We can leave the high notes to the girls. But how did it feel to get the low notes out from way down in your chest? Was this more comfortable?"

"Much more comfortable. Those growling sounds are more to my liking. They make me feel fierce."

This observation made Mama Mouse laugh. Soon Morris joined in.

"Growling is not exactly what we want you to do. It's a beginning. But now you have to mellow those sounds a bit. Get out more melodic deep tones. Try! And listen to Morris. He managed to become a very good tenor. But you, dear, will make a strong bass. Trust me."

Morris was happy to demonstrate his technique to his father, and, honestly, he sounded better than ever before.

Papa Mouse, fearing ridicule, finally decided not to treat his family's singing business as a joke anymore, and from that moment on, he tried, really tried, to produce more pleasant squeaks. And how proud he was when he managed going from real low to a bit higher and higher and higher. Morris and Mama

Mouse could hardly believe the range he developed in such a short time.

"Let's harmonize," Morris suggested, and Mama Mouse nodded vigorously in agreement.

They did.

The girls, though rehearsing a good distance away, heard the improvised song. It sounded so beautiful they had to follow the source to make sure it was really coming from Mama, Papa and Morris.

It's a miracle, Mollie thought. *Who would ever have dared to imagine …"* And then she turned to Millie, Marcie and Emmie and said, "We better get back to practice. Marcie still has to learn an awful lot, and Emmie, though she is already pretty good, can do a lot better. Actually, we all could use much more practice. We are not perfect yet. After having heard our parents and Morris harmonize, we know we have plenty of catching up to do."

"Practice, practice, practice," Millie mumbled. "More practice."

"This isn't how I had imagined my sleepover with you," Marcie groused. "Not at all."

"And I never imagined my visit here would turn out like this. But … I like it." To prove her delight, Emmie let out some beautiful trills.

"Wow!" Marcie exclaimed. "How did you do that?"

"Put your mind to it. Think it. Up there, high in your head. Then let the sound come out."

Marcie tried. The miracle happened. The other three mice joined in, and they began to dance, all the while happily singing. And that's how Mama Mouse, Papa Mouse and Morris, returning from their side of the tunnel, caught them.

"All right, girls, this is beautiful," Mama Mouse exclaimed. "You did well. We all did well. And now, what do you think about calling it a night and going to sleep?"

Reluctantly, the four girls found a cozy sleeping spot, close together, and Morris lay down a bit off to the side.

Mama Mouse and Papa Mouse stayed awake a little longer, because they had so much to tell each other, especially how proud they were of their children.

The People Choir

"Marcie, Marcie, wake up!"

"What is it, Mollie?"

"You said you wanted to listen to the people choir. We have to get upstairs, into the church, before the people arrive. Then we have to hide in a spot where they cannot see us."

"I know. And we have to be quiet."

"What are you whispering about?" Millie, still half asleep, asked.

"Don't you remember why Marcie came to us?" Mollie shook her head, wondering how her sister could have forgotten. "She wanted to sneak into the church with me."

"Do you want me to come along? I would like to listen to what is going on upstairs, too."

"Okay. Get yourself up and let's go. And no noise, please."

Soon, the three young mice were out of the hole, crossed the kitchen, made their way upstairs, and found a corner toward the front of the church, where there were some small boxes and other assorted paraphernalia that hid them well enough. That's where they waited for the service to begin. The people choir sat not far from their hiding place.

At first, they heard beautiful music played on a big instrument that looked somewhat like the neglected piano in the downstairs room, but it was a lot fancier. The man in the white robe said a few things. All the people responded. Then they all sang. Other people said something. More singing. And then, finally, the choir had its turn.

The three hidden mice were so impressed, especially Marcie, who began to open her mouth to let out a heartfelt squeak. Mollie quickly hushed her.

When the man in white gave a long talk, the mice paid close attention. They loved to hear the story about Christmas coming and people waiting for the birth of the baby boy, the savior of the world.

"What is a savior?" Millie whispered.

"I don't know," Mollie whispered back. Marcie just shrugged, for she, too, did not know the answer.

The church service dragged on and on, and the three little mice got mighty tired of listening. But they did not dare to abandon their hiding place until the last people person had left the building.

When they got back to their hole, Mama Mouse was there, anxiously waiting for them. She looked cross and asked, "Where have you three been? Sneaking off without letting me know was naughty. I was worried."

"We were upstairs in the church, listening."

"And … was it worth the heart attack you almost gave me?"

"Yes, Mama, it was very nice. But we didn't want you to have a heart attack, whatever that is."

"Oh, never mind, children. Now that you have returned and are safe and sound I am all right. But at least tell me what you have learned."

And that was exactly what Mollie, Millie and Marcie did. They did not leave out a thing. What they bragged about most was the people choir. And the nice sound of the big instrument that looked more impressive than the old piano.

"It would be so lovely to have some instrument to accompany our singing." Mollie let out a big sigh. "It would be so nice."

"Perhaps … we can … figure out something," Mama Mouse said. "I have to seriously think about it."

"Dear Mama, we trust you will come up with something," Millie said. "You are so clever. You always have wonderful ideas."

"We will see. Yes, we will see." And Mama Mouse began to think very hard immediately.

Help Is on the Way

Getting to the next rehearsal in the woodshed was no problem. The church seemed perfectly empty. Nobody was in the kitchen. No janitor doing his chores. And if people were in a different section of the building, they went undetected by the mice.

Outside, it was even colder than the day before. Snow had fallen during the night, but just enough to put a very thin blanket over everything.

"Look at all our footprints!" Marcie exclaimed excitedly. "I've never seen so many together. How could I have? I've never experienced snow before."

"Neither have we, I mean Morris, Mollie and I, and definitely not Emmie.

Emmie was born after us." Millie knew that snow only fell in the cold winter months, because Mama Mouse had explained it to her before, when they had moved from their outdoor place into the warm hole in the church.

They arrived at a section of the field where the ground sloped down a bit, and to everyone's amazement, Papa Mouse suddenly broke away from their cluster and skittered ahead. Then … what was he doing? He put himself on his back and … whoosh! … slid down, laughing all the way. When he got up again, he called to the others, "Now you try it!"

Morris was first, and he shouted, "Wheeee … wow … ha, ha, ha!"

The others followed, Mama Mouse last. It was so much fun. And then they shook the snow off their backs and continued on their way to the woodshed.

When they were about to enter the shed, they found Marcie's parents waiting for them. After having inspected their daughter to make sure she was unharmed, they thanked Mama and Papa Mouse for having had their little girl over at their place, and then they said, "Before going in, we want to tell you something important."

"What is it?" Papa Mouse asked.

"We have seen a visitor lurking around here. A big, fat rat. He seems peaceful enough. Should we confront him and ask what he wants?"

"Hmm … let me think." And Papa Mouse was thinking.

In the meantime, Mama Mouse shooed the youngsters inside, because she believed it would be better to have just the grownups around to deal with the rat visitor.

Papa Mouse had made up his mind. Yes, it would be best to go to the rat and find out why he was there and what he wanted.

A moment later, the four adult mice confronted the stranger with their questions.

"I listened to your rehearsal, and I was amazed. Never before did I hear mice singing. It made me want to sing along. My voice would be too loud for your choir, though. If I could only do something to be part of the group."

"Perhaps you can help us think. Your brain is bigger than ours," Papa Mouse suggested.

"Thank you," the rat said. "Tell me what you want me to think about."

"Our little Mollie said that the people choir in the church has some kind of instrument bigger than a piano, which, when it is played, makes the singing sound even better. We mice don't have such an instrument to accompany our singers, and we have not come up with an idea of what we could use to produce nice sounds to enhance our singing. We would value any suggestion, Mr. Rat."

"You are looking for something that makes music, pretty music?" The rat began to laugh.

"Why do you laugh?" Mama Mouse asked. "Do you think our idea is too ridiculous?"

"No, no, my dear mouse, your idea is fantastic. I laugh because the solution is so very easy."

"If you think it is so easy, then please tell us, Mr. Rat."

"I guess you don't know where I live. It's at the dump. And if you have never been to a dump, then you don't know what wonderful stuff people throw there. When you live in a dump, you live like a king. You find everything you need and much more. You are looking for a thing or things that makes music, I've got it. I can bring you a small bell that makes tinkling sounds, and then there's a small toy instrument that has a number of thin metal pieces of different sizes, and when you hit on those metal pieces, they make different sounds. Just like you mice produce different tones when you sing. This fancy toy instrument, if I remember correctly, is called a … ah! … a xylophone. I guess you could compare it with a piano, just not as big."

"Oh, my goodness!" Mama Mouse exclaimed, and the other three mice stood with their mouths wide open in wonderment.

"But how could we bring those nice instruments here? They are, I am sure, much too big and heavy for us mice," Papa Mouse said.

"Problem solved." The rat nodded vehemently, and his whiskers shook like crazy. "I have friends. Good friends. They would be only too glad to help you. And I even know a few pals, who would gladly play the instruments for you, if you let them. Rowdy would probably like to ring the bell. Racine, a young female and very talented, oh, yes, she would, I am sure, love to play the xylophone. Should I bring my good friends and the instruments tomorrow? To this place?"

"Please do!" all four mice shouted in unison. "And thank you, Mr. Rat."

"Would you like to stay for today's rehearsal?" Mama Mouse asked. "We could introduce you to our friends and neighbors and tell them you are now officially a member of our group."

"That's wonderful. I may even learn something about singing."

Of course, when all five entered the woodshed, the assembled singers had no idea what was going on. What was a big, fat rat doing in their midst? Some were afraid and thought of leaving the gathering.

"Stop! Don't run away!" shouted Papa Mouse. "You have nothing to fear. This big fellow here is Mr. Rat, our new friend, and he and a few of his fellow rats are going to assist us with our Christmas concert. Imagine! They will use musical instruments to accompany our choir. Isn't this great?"

Instead of instant applause from everyone, which Papa Mouse had expected, only a few showed approval. The rest of them gave doubtful looks and made all kinds of questioning remarks. "Musical instruments?" "Isn't singing enough?" "Accompany our nice choir?" "Rats joining us for our concert?" "Has the church mouse family gone crazy?"

"Believe me, my good friends," Papa Mouse continued, "once you hear the combination of your voices and the instruments, you will all agree that what we are doing is not just novel but also wonderful, and you will want to repeat it again and again. But now we really have to begin our rehearsal or nothing will be accomplished. Into your corners, please, sopranos, altos, tenors and basses. And I hope you have all practiced and gotten your voices into good shape."

And so the sopranos gathered around Mollie and Millie, the female mice with the somewhat lower voices joined Mama Mouse, the males of the tenor group flocked around Morris, and the men who could only manage the bass notes huddled near Papa Mouse and waited for the cue to show their progress.

A few mice had to be reprimanded for not having practiced, and they were warned that they would be eliminated from the choir should they not do what was required of them.

"This is not just a social gathering," Mama Mouse said. "We are here to sing, and singing needs practice. Lots of practice. I hope you all understand this."

The mice nodded, and then they tried extra hard to please their leader, Mama Mouse.

At the end of the practice meeting, it was decided that, since everything seemed to be progressing well, the four groups might be ready to harmonize. Bits by little bits, each section would be taught the melody, which Mollie already had in her mind.

"Don't worry," Mollie said. "We will take it slowly."

Then she turned to a mouse named Mattie and asked, "Would you mind switching to my mama's section? I think the lower alto notes would be easier for you. It's not a demotion, really. Altos are just as important as sopranos, and I myself love the sound of alto voices."

"All right, Mollie, I will gladly switch to alto. Then I may not have to strain so terribly." Mattie gave a relieved sigh and happily scampered to Mama Mouse's corner.

"May I switch to soprano and join Mollie?" Alex asked.

"No, Alex. You have been told before you can't do it. Boys don't sing soprano. Girls do." Mama Mouse sounded cross. *I know exactly what is going on. This young fellow likes my Mollie, and he is trying very hard to be near her.*

Alex sulked for a little while and then joined his parents, who were ready to go home.

"Well, Mr. Rat, how did you like our rehearsal?" Papa Mouse asked. "Do you still want to bring your friends with the instruments?'

"Indeed, I will bring them, and they will love the rehearsals as much as I do. Good night."

Oh, What a Night!

With joy in their hearts, the mouse children scurried ahead of Mama and Papa Mouse across the field. The last of the daylight had vanished; stars were out; the temperature had dropped. What used to be a powdery snow cover had frozen into sheets of solid ice. Soon the youngsters found out that the smooth surface was good for sliding. Their first attempts ended up in short, gentle gliding. Then, using more force, they managed long slides.

"This is fun!" they shouted.

Off and on, one of the girls would lose her balance and land on her side, and when this happened, Morris shook with laughter.

"Watch me!" he called for everybody to hear. "I will show you some tricks." Instead of just sliding forward, the fellow changed directions and finally attempted a full spin. But … something went badly wrong. He teetered. He fell. After a few not-so-graceful rolls, he ended up flat on his back, all four legs pointing skyward. It was a comical sight to behold.

Before Mama and Papa Mouse could get to their son, the girls were there already, trying to help him up. But before they rolled him over, Millie grabbed his stubby tail, pulled it hard, and caused Morris to slide more. He was still on his back, of course. The unexpected movement made Mollie and Emmie lose their balance, too. And in a flash, three little mice were flat on the ice.

Morris, not pleased at all, began to holler, "You dummies, you miserable bunch of girls, get away from me! Mama, Papa, help!"

Instead of being mad, Mama and Papa Mouse had a hearty laugh first, and only when they were done laughing, did they come to the aid of their son.

"See what you got from trying to show off?" Papa Mouse stood at his son's side and giggled. "You, dear boy, made a spectacle of yourself. And, honestly, you could have rolled over by yourself. Don't always play helpless. You are not a baby anymore."

Then Mama Mouse got her say. It was directed at the girls. "I am also disappointed in you. All of you. What you did to Morris was not nice."

"Sorry. We are really sorry," they said.

"I'm going to pay you back," Morris hissed.

"No, you won't, son," Papa Mouse warned. "I will not hear of it."

"It was such a nice rehearsal, and now this." Mama Mouse gave a deep sigh.

"Oh, forget about what has just happened, dear," Papa Mouse said to his wife. "Let's only concentrate on the progress we made. And don't forget to be thankful for the friendship we began with Mr. Rat."

"You are correct, my wise husband." Then Mama Mouse smiled again, and all was right with the world.

Stars and …

"Look at the beautiful stars, dear," Mama Mouse said to her husband and gave him a loving bump on the right shoulder. "The sky is so clear tonight, and the stars seem extra bright. I am so glad we happen to be outdoors tonight."

Papa Mouse stood still and looked all around. He had to agree that he had never seen such a clear night sky before. Some of the stars appeared to be winking at him as if to say hello.

Because the children noticed that the parents had stopped and were staring at the stars, they did the same.

"I wonder what it is like up there." Mollie looked thoughtful. "I wonder if the stars look down and watch us. And will they, perhaps, be listening to our nice Christmas choir?"

"Don't be silly, Mollie." Morris shook his head.

"You have no imagination, my dear brother," Millie reprimanded him.

"Let me share something with you," Emmie butted in. "I have three brothers at home, and they always contradict whatever I am saying. I guess that's how it is, brothers always think they are smarter than their sisters, but it isn't so."

Morris shook his head again. He thought it would be better to keep his thoughts to himself instead of getting into an argument with the girls. There were three of them, and three against one was not favorable. Also, Mama and Papa might get upset and give everyone a good tongue lashing. *Not again, not tonight,* he thought and walked away.

"Hush!" Papa Mouse suddenly called out, just loud enough for his family to hear. "I believe there's danger coming. It sounds like something flying in the air. I

cannot see it yet, but my ears heard …
what could it be?"

"There, in the distance, coming this
way. A hawk. Hide, everybody hide.
Quickly!" Mama Mouse's voice betrayed
great alarm.

"Hide where?" the children's voices
screeched.

"Under this rock there," Papa Mouse
ordered. "Follow me!"

It was sheer luck that a big enough
rock was nearby under which all six
mice could find shelter. It was a tight fit,
but what did it matter?

"Hawks come out at night and look
for prey," Mama Mouse explained. They
look for small animals. One of us mice
would make a tasty meal for that hawk. I
am glad Papa paid attention and heard
it coming."

"That's so scary," Emmie whispered.
"I think I want to go home to my own
family. I feel safer there."

"You can't," Mollie said. "You have to
stay until our singing is over. You can't
miss all the fun."

"You are right, Mollie. I'll stick it out here. And, besides, I wouldn't want to miss the instruments Mr. Rat promised to bring. This will be so exciting."

"I hope he will show up," Morris mumbled.

"You pessimist," Mollie chided him. "You'll see, he will be at our rehearsal tomorrow. You'll see."

"Right now I don't care. I want to be back in the church kitchen and find food. I'm starving."

Papa Mouse had listened in on the conversation. He, too, felt slight hunger pangs. Carefully, he stuck his head out from under the rock, and when he heard no sound of a big bird, he motioned his family to come out. It would be safe to go home.

Surprise

The following evening, after a stiff warning from Papa Mouse to be extra careful when crossing the ice covered parking lot, the mouse family, with the children close behind their parents, raced through the seemingly empty church building and out into the open. But instead of a hard, smooth, slippery surface, they found slush in the parking lot. This meant the sun had been out during the day and melted the ice.

Though the much warmer evening temperature pleased everyone, crossing the lot was more difficult.

"Try to avoid the big puddles," Mama Mouse told her children. "Getting wet bellies is no fun. Not in the winter."

"But in the summer, when it's warm."

"Just listen to your mother," Papa Mouse warned and tried to find the safest way around an especially large puddle.

Naughty Morris, however, stomped extra hard and laughed when the water splashed so high that it hit his nose. When his father gave him a stern look, he shrank back and did not dare to perform the act a second time.

"Is your brother always bad?" Emmie asked Mollie.

"No, only sometimes," her cousin answered. "It's a boy thing. Boys like to show off. They also want to see what they can get away with."

"I guess you are right. My brothers also get into trouble off and on."

Crossing the big field gave the mice wet paws, but the ground had already absorbed most of the water from the melted ice and snow.

"Yesterday was much more fun." Millie let out a small sigh.

Mollie, Morris and Emmie agreed.

When they reached the woodshed, as if by order, all came to a sudden standstill. They looked at each other. They could not believe what they heard. This was not music played by a people band. People made loud noises. This was much softer. Not exactly perfect harmony. More like a practice session with each musician doing his own thing.

"This must be Mr. Rat's doing," Papa Mouse suddenly said. "How many of his friends did he bring along? Let's check it out."

So they all rushed to get closer, and what did they find? There was Mr. Rat, a tiny party hat on his head, directing a bell ringer – no, three bell ringers – a trumpeter, a drummer, and one wildly banging on a piano-like gadget called a xylophone. And in a semicircle behind the rat musicians, a bunch of mice huddled to listen to the dissonant concert.

"Those critters are not going to ruin my Christmas music!" Mollie screamed. "No way! We mice are doing quite well already, but these rats, they make an awful noise. I would never call their instrumental racket music."

"But, child, don't judge in haste." Mama Mouse knew she had to do something to calm her brood. "Don't you remember what we sounded like in the beginning? Awful. Everything needs practice."

"Yes, practice, practice, and more practice." Mollie gave a few serious nods. "I remember your words."

Chaos

"What have you brought us, Mr. Rat?" Papa Mouse asked after having reached the leader of the band and greeted him.

"I hope you don't mind that we are so many," the rat replied. "But when I told my friends about your choir and the idea of instruments accompanying the singers, they all wanted to be part of it. So, in a great hurry, they ran to the spot where we had seen those small toy music makers. You should have seen my rat friends! They were so eager. But when we got to that certain spot, we discovered that another load of trash had been dumped on top of those toys. Of course, we were disappointed. But giving up? No way! We dug and dug, and finally we found what we wanted. And here we are now, ready to be of service."

"That's wonderful," Papa Mouse said. "And please tell all your friends that we appreciate their coming. But I have to ask you something."

"Go ahead and ask."

"Do you think they will be willing to practice to get the melody right? Not to drown us out? To make it sound nice and harmonious?"

"But of course. Don't worry. They will learn to follow my direction, and I have a pretty good ear for music."

"I trust you, Mr. Rat."

Then Papa Mouse turned to the assembly of mice and rats and said, "Let's move into the woodshed now and begin our rehearsal. As usual, first each section in its own corner, then all of us together. Mr. Rat may want to choose his rehearsal place somewhere in the back, and when we mice are ready to let the sections sing together, we will call the instrumentalists to come and listen to us. Then they get an idea of what our melody sounds like, and they can figure out what to do."

That's exactly how it was handled. All went according to plan … until the eager rats tried to accompany the singers.

The trumpet fanfare was fantastic. So impressed were some of the singers that they forgot their entrance. The tinkling of the bells provided a pleasant background, but the young girl rat playing the xylophone was overdoing it with her stick and often hit the keys too hard and not in the best sequence. For good measure, toward the end, she also jumped onto her instrument and, kind of dancing, hit the keys wherever her feet landed.

And the drummer? He enjoyed his instrument so very much that he kept banging and banging to whatever rhythm pleased him at the moment.

The trumpeter, not knowing when his part was needed, joined in any time he felt like.

It was chaos, sheer chaos.

The singers had given up a long time before the "orchestra" paid attention to Mr. Rat, its illustrious conductor, and finally stopped.

Mollie cried. Millie and Emmie were too stunned to do anything. Morris dared to laugh. And Mama and Papa Mouse stared at each other and shook their heads.

"I'm so very sorry," Mr. Rat said after his musician friends had stopped the noise. "Really sorry. But believe me, I know how to correct it."

"How?" Papa and Mama Mouse asked in unison.

"Please let your mouse choir sing the melody again. We will listen. I have an excellent memory. Then I will escort my group out of here and back to the dump, where I will drill them until they know exactly what to do. I promise that, if you allow us to come back tomorrow, you will not be disappointed in us."

"Okay, we will give it another try." Papa Mouse hoped he had made the right decision.

As soon as the rats, with all their instruments, had left the woodshed, the singers rehearsed a while longer. It sounded a lot better without the rats' wild instrumental accompaniment.

Too Much Activity

"What is all that noise above us?" Emmie asked. "So much trampling, thumping, things dropping, and people's voices. They sound happy. They talk and talk, and they laugh and sing. Honestly, I have never heard so much going on in the house where I live."

"If you would stay here with us long enough, you would get used to the occasional busy activities upstairs." Mollie, who had been resting next to her cousin, had to smile at little Emmie's observation. She knew that, whenever the church people were getting ready for a celebration, there was much activity in the kitchen and in the storage room.

Normally, she had no idea what the people were celebrating, but she knew what it was this time. No doubt, it was the birthday of that long awaited baby boy on Christmas Day long, long ago. How could she ever forget the words of the man dressed in white? How could she forget what the people choir had been singing about for the last few weeks? That big day must be near, and the people were getting ready for it.

"I hope they leave a lot of crumbs on the floor," Morris remarked.

"And I hope they will get out before we have to leave for rehearsal," Mama Mouse said.

Millie whimpered. "I'm scared."

Mama Mouse bent down and gently nuzzled her niece's head, cooing, "Don't be, little one. As long as we are quiet and don't show ourselves to the people, everything will be fine. We are safe down her."

"Do you think we can hum, softly, Mama?" Mollie asked. "We could use the practice. And when we hum, not sing out loud, it may soothe our nerves."

"Good idea, Mollie," Mama Mouse answered. "But only softly. "

And this they did to pass the time until, all of a sudden, no more noise from upstairs could be heard. For safety, they waited and listened carefully for a long time, and then Papa Mouse, with great caution, ventured out of the hole.

Not a single person was downstairs. All activity had been moved to upstairs. Papa Mouse could tell, for sounds came only from a faraway area of the building, on a higher floor.

Papa Mouse gave the signal for his family to come out, and because it was still much too early to leave for choir rehearsal, they had plenty of time to gorge themselves on the absolutely delicious food scraps there for the taking. What a feast they had!

Well fed, they began to explore. They especially focused their attention on the vicinity of the storage closet. That's where they found an interesting trail of glittering stuff, tinsel, and even a few tiny, shiny, colorful decorations. Mama and Papa knew what they were, for they had already experienced a previous Christmas.

"This is what people put on trees to make them look pretty," Mama Mouse explained.

"May we pick up some of the glittery strands to decorate our place?" Millie asked.

"May we?" the other children joined in the plea.

"Why not?" Mama Mouse said.

Then Papa Mouse put a strand on Mama Mouse, and because it looked so nice, the children dropped some on themselves, too.

"Let's decorate Papa," Morris suggested.

With a lot of laughter, they did, but Papa Mouse shook it off. Most of it.

For that, Mama Mouse chided him. "Don't you understand fun, you old grey mouse?"

Papa Mouse shook his head and grinned. Then he said, "Let's go. It's time to be on our way to meet our friends in the woodshed."

It's All Good

When our decorated church mice marched across the parking lot, it looked like a holiday parade. Papa Mouse led his family. Mama Mouse was behind, and following, in single file, were Morris, Mollie, Millie and Emmie. Each time the light from a lamp in the parking lot fell on them, the tinsel glittered beautifully.

Mama Mouse was first to discover the sparkling on her husband's back, and when she turned to look at the children behind her, her eyes opened wide in amazement. Never before had she seen such a sight. Glittering silver streaks moving along. It made her a bit giddy, and she began to sing. Soon, the song was picked up by all.

Adding to the joyous feeling was the fact that the ground was dry. All wetness from previous days' melted ice and snow had disappeared. Crossing the parking lot was easy, and even the walk across the field, frozen now, gave the mice no wet and muddy feet.

When they reached the woodshed, a number of their fellow singers were already waiting. Reception was mixed. Some looked in wonderment, others laughed, and a few curious youngsters came running to examine the tinsel more closely. One even dared to touch it, sighed, and said, "I wish I could have some, too."

"Take a bit off me and give it to her," Papa Mouse said to his wife. She did and gave it to the little one.

"Thank you, thank you," squeaked the small mouse and then affectionately rubbed her shoulder against Papa and Mama Mouse.

Priscilla was about to approach Papa Mouse, too, and ask for a bit of the glittery strands, but her mother held her back and chided her for her tendency to be vain.

"Oh, Mama," Priscilla said and walked away, pouting. In no time at all, she was back, because the rat band was entering.

Please let this work out, was on every mouse's mind, and one mouse in the back even said it out loud.

Here Comes the Band

Every instrumentalist's face radiated confidence as Mr. Rat, again wearing his funny hat, escorted his band into the woodshed. All members dragged their instruments behind them, because those things were too big and heavy to carry a long distance. The singers had it easier, for their instruments, the vocal cords, were already in their throats.

"We practiced," Mr. Rat told Papa Mouse as they exchanged greetings.

"That's wonderful, my friend," Papa Mouse answered.

Mama Mouse joined them, and after letting the leader of the band know how happy she was that he kept his word and came back with his friends, she explained the order for this evening's rehearsal. "You and your musicians first listen to the singers. Then you take your rats to the far corner again to practice. Our singers will also practice. After that, we will put all members together and continue rehearsing. Okay?"

Before Mr. Rat had a chance to answer, Mollie, who had listened in, interrupted. "Excuse me for butting in, but I don't think it is as easy as this. That's not how it is done. The players have to know when it is their time to come in. They cannot toot and bang away whenever they please. It would ruin everything."

"Then, my child, what do you have in mind?"

"Yes, it is already clear in my mind how it is supposed to be."

"Tell us. I am sure Mr. Rat, Papa and I would benefit from your suggestions. You, after all, have been listening to the church choir, and then you got it into your head that you wanted your own. "

"This was a child's idea? I didn't know." Mr. Rat was amazed. "What is your name?"

"My name is Mollie. And what's your name, if I may ask?"

"Call me Mr. Rat like the others do. But, actually, my full name is Roderic Ramondo Rat. That's much too long and complicated for anybody to remember. So … Mr. Rat it is."

Mollie giggled. Then she asked, "Do you want me to give you my ideas right now or later?"

"Right now would be the best," Mama Mouse decided, and the others agreed.

"Here it is. A big trumpet fanfare. Then a drumroll, no trumpet. A moment of silence. The bells begin to ring, ever so softly, and the choir joins in. When I give the cue, the xylophone starts to accompany the singers, following the rhythm of our song. Off and on the bells come in a gain. There will be a slight pause in the singing, and the trumpet sounds again. The singers come in with the xylophone, and the drummer gently pounds out the beat. Suddenly, we get louder. It has to be really joyful. All instruments, strong sound – except for the xylophone, finish the performance. My mother will give Mr. Rat a cue, and he will give his orchestra friends the cut-off sign. No stragglers. All stop together. That's the only way it will be effective. Is that clear?"

Mr. Rat and Mollie's parents nodded.

"And now let's get started." Mama Mouse ordered. "Our friends are already getting restless."

Indeed they were. They had no idea what the discussion up front was about. Some even talked of wanting to go home, though they dismissed this thought as soon as Mama Mouse turned around to explain.

"I'm very sorry for the big delay, but we had to let helpful Mr. Rat know what we expected of his band. And I want to announce that we have just made Mollie co-director of the choir. She will help direct the band … and the choir. She's the only one who really knows how it's supposed to work."

There were loud cheers, and then rehearsal began in earnest.

Did everything turn out as expected? Of course not. It would have been a surprise if it did. All things need practice, practice, and more practice.

The drummer was too loud when he was supposed to just gently but steadily beat the rhythm. The bells were a tad too timid, and the xylophonist didn't pay attention to the cues.

"Maybe not everybody got to see me," Mollie suggested. "Could someone perhaps push a stack of little boards over here so I can climb on them and be higher up?"

Because they were stronger, the rats did it, and Mollie thanked them.

"One more try please, right from the beginning," Mama Mouse said.

With Mollie on her new high podium, there was no excuse for anyone not to see her. And … what miracle … the sound of orchestra and choir together had improved tremendously. There was great hope they would be concert-ready in a few days.

Owl Attack

"This has truly been an interesting session," the old mouse said. "You can't imagine how much pleasure it has provided me to come here to listen to your choir rehearsals. Mollie, dear child, I applaud you for having had this idea."

"I'm so glad you could always come, Mrs. Moss," Mollie replied. "It's too bad you can't sing with us. When you were younger, you probably had a pretty voice, too. I bet you would've been a soprano."

"Perhaps. I'll never know. But I have to go now, Mollie. My friend is waiting to see me home. It's good I don't have far to go. My old legs are as tired as my voice."

"Have a safe trip home, Mrs. Moss. I hope to see you tomorrow. But be very careful in case it gets icy out there like a few days ago. I don't want you to slip and hurt yourself."

"You are such a sweet girl, Mollie. And so talented."

"Thank you, Mrs. Moss."

Mollie watched as the old mouse was being led out of the woodshed by her friend. *Nice old mouse,* she thought, and then she went to rejoin her family.

She passed Millie and Emmie, who were still talking and giggling with some friends, and then she saw Morris in a corner, surrounded by a group of girls. He seemed to be the center of their attention.

Not long ago, they were bullying him, making fun of his shortened tail and funny ear, and now they can't get close enough to him, she thought. *Singing has worked wonders.*

Mama and Papa Mouse were still in deep conversation with Mr. Rat, and

Mollie wondered how much longer it would be until they could all go home.

Suddenly, terrible shrieks could be heard from just outside the woodshed. Moments later, several mice, barely out of the building, came running back in.

"An owl! Big danger! Stay indoors! If you don't want to be eaten, don't go out there!"

Warnings were sounded from many mice, and Mollie could not distinguish who shouted what. She thought of the old mouse, who had just left with her companion, and she was worried. "I hope Mrs. Moss made it home safely," she whispered. It was almost like a prayer.

Priscilla, who had been one of the returning, was hysterical. Her parents tried to comfort her, assuring her that she was now safely back in the old woodshed and surrounded by friends, but nothing they said could stop her tears and her shaking. She would not calm down until Morris put his paw on her and crooned to her in a soothing way.

Mr. Rat, finally aware of the big commotion, asked, "What is going on? Why all this shrieking and wailing?"

"An owl, on the prowl, looking for food, looking for mice to eat," he was informed.

"I will take care of that," Mr. Rat said and made himself look even bigger than he was. Then he called his musicians and told them what to do. Since he did not give his orders loud enough for the mice to hear, they wondered what he was up to. And when they saw two of the rats, dragging their instruments, running for the door, they really believed Mr. Rat and his friends had gone crazy.

Big drum banging and loud trumpet sounds could soon be heard. It was an earsplitting noise that went on for a long time. And when it finally stopped, two totally exhausted rats, the drummer and the trumpeter, hit the ground. It took a while for them to recover.

"Well done, my friends," Mr. Rat said. "You chased the owl away. Now everybody will be able to go home." *And the owl may starve to death,* he thought, *for food is very rare for owls in the cold winter.*

All mice applauded, and then they thanked Mr. Rat and his brave friends a thousand times. Their joy was not totally complete until the companion of Mrs. Moss came back to report that her good friend, the old mouse, had made it to her home, safely, and was now recovering from her scare.

"I should have left with my father," Emmie said in a small voice. "Too many frightening things are happening here."

"No, you shouldn't," Mollie whispered back. "You would have missed out on a lot of wonderful things. Remember, you would have never learned how to sing. You would not have known about rats making music. And you would not have learned about a tiny baby boy born on Christmas Day."

"I guess you are right again, Mollie. You always manage to make me feel better."

"Okay, children, what do you think about us going home now?" Papa Mouse said as he neared with Mama Mouse by his side.

And home they went … without any bad encounter.

Ready for the Show

The next few rehearsals went without troubling incidents. Each day, improvements were noticeable, and the comradery between mice and rats was a sheer joy to behold. They encouraged and applauded each other until, finally, they performed so well together that Mollie exclaimed, "That's it! We've done it. We are ready for the show."

Mama and Papa Mouse agreed, and Mr. Rat was so happy that he danced a little jig, which made his party hat slip off and fall to the ground. Everybody had a good laugh.

"So, when can we have our lovely concert?" one mouse asked.

"Tomorrow," a youngster suggested.

"Please, please, tomorrow," others chimed in.

"And where?"

"On the town square?"

"In the big church?"

"In the same place where we had the talent show?"

Everybody was full of suggestions, but Papa and Mama Mouse liked none of them.

"It's too dangerous for so many of us to meet in public places. And don't you remember the cats that would have liked to have us for a tasty dinner after the talent show? That place is too close to the cats." Mama shook her head with vehemence.

"And we certainly cannot have our choir perform tomorrow. I say, that's too soon. We want an audience. And this needs publicity." Papa Mouse paused for a moment, then he continued. "I think we all have to do our part when it comes to spreading the word. Even to the mice in neighboring towns. I myself will make a trip to tell Emmie's folks about it, and they can spread the word to their friends and neighbors. They live in another town, you know, and it will take me a few days to return. The same thing will be true for many of you."

At first, the announcement caused some grumbling among the mice, but then they voiced their support.

"This woodshed is large. It will hold a big audience. Also, we have been safe in here. No cats visiting, no dogs, and no people. I suggest that we will have everybody come to this shed to listen to our wonderful Christmas choir." Papa Mouse looked around to see what the reaction might be to his suggestion. He saw a lot of nodding.

"I guess it's all settled now about the location," he said. "But what about the date?"

"In one week from now," Mama Mouse decided. "Don't forget to spread the word. And, most of all, don't forget to practice at home. This goes for our rat friends, too. And, this is very important, one day before the performance we all have to meet here for a final rehearsal. Let's hope for good weather. We don't want to get stuck in the snow."

"Please, no deep snow," Mr. Rat said. "My friends would have a hard time dragging their big instruments through heavy white stuff."

"Everybody listen!" Mollie suddenly called out. "I have an idea. Perhaps you will like it."

"Tell us," Mama Mouse said. "Climb up on your podium so all can see and hear you better."

Mollie did just that, and then she began, "You all know that we, my family, live in a church. I have watched the people who always come in there to listen to the man in the white robe and to the choir. On special occasions, the people don't go right home. They stay and celebrate with food and drink. Now I've been thinking. We, too, are going to come together for a special occasion. Why can't we, also, celebrate with food after the concert? Like the people do in the church."

"And who would provide all the food for our celebration?" one mouse asked.

"I watched the church people bring in food. Then they shared. Don't you think sharing is good?" Mollie looked at the gathered mice. Confidence showed on her face.

"If you can scrounge around for much, bring much to share. But if the pickings at your place are slim, then you cannot help it. But come anyhow." Again, Mollie looked around, trying to figure out what the reaction to her speech might be.

It took a while until she heard the first tentative agreement. Soon, others followed. At the end, most of the mice joyfully agreed to do their best.

"I call this success," Papa Mouse said. He gave the impression as if he had accomplished it all.

Mr. Rat threw him a disapproving glance. Then he looked him squarely in the eyes and said, "You better not take all the credit, my friend. It is mostly your daughter, Mollie, who deserves it. She is the smart one, the one with all the good ideas and the know-how. Without her, and I hope you agree, we could not have accomplished a thing. And you better remember that your wife worked very hard, too, to bring this all together. She was the main organizer."

At first, Papa Mouse thought he should take offense and considered giving a nasty response. But before his words had a chance to tumble out, he felt a warning kick from Mama Mouse, and he heard her whisper, "Cool it, dear. Mr. Rat made a point. Think about it."

So … Papa Mouse swallowed hard, held his tongue, and thought about the matter for a few moments. Then he looked at Mr. Rat and said, "You are correct. Thank you for reminding me. We men have a tendency to believe that we are the strong ones, the backbones of our families, the ones who possess brains. We rarely give our wives and our children, and especially our daughters, enough credit."

Mr. Rat nodded. He knew it was the same in the rat society. He himself used to belong to the group of males with inflated egos. Not until his beloved mate was taken away from him by a tragic accident did he realize how little he had valued her talents. Then he wished he had given her some praise before it was too late. Those sad memories almost brought him to tears. So he quickly said goodbye to the mice and crept back to the dump, to his lonely home. *At least I have friends,* he thought. *And now I have a new purpose in life, something that really cheers me up. I am the leader of a newly founded band – or call it an orchestra, if this sounds better. Music is good for the soul. For the music maker and for the listener. And right now, I am really looking forward to little Mollie's Christmas choir, accompanied by my rat friends.*

Papa Mouse Is Important

On the way home from rehearsal, Mama Mouse felt sorry for her husband. By looking at him, she knew his ego had been crushed by Mr. Rat's harsh words. She was a caring wife, and she wanted to see him happy.

For a while, the grownups trotted home in silence. Even the children were unusually quiet. It just did not feel right.

Suddenly, Mama Mouse had an idea. *He needs a pep talk,* she thought. *I know how to restore his feeling of being important. And come to think of it, he will play a very important part in the next few days.*

So Mama Mouse sidled up to her mate and began to talk. "The coming days will be taxing for you. It's such a long walk to your sister's house. And then back again in time to make the final rehearsal. I am so proud of you to have agreed to this extremely important undertaking. I hope you will be able to talk your sister and her husband into coming to hear Emmie sing, and I hope they will agree to spread the word about the performance among their friends and neighbors. And, please, don't forget to mention that we will have food after the show, and that we asked everybody to contribute to the feast. This is going to be a sharing event. Why should only humans have all the fun? We mice will create our own Christmas celebration. And in case they ask what you are talking about, you will know what to say. You've heard it from Mollie. It's about the birth of that special baby boy from a long time ago."

"I know." Papa Mouse sighed. "To tell the truth, I'm not looking forward to the long walk and all this explaining. But … I will do it for Mollie and for you and for all those involved in the program. I guess that's the least I can do. And I don't want to listen to a big speech from Mr. Rat again. I have to prove to him that I am a caring husband and father and not a spoiled male mouse with a big ego."

"I know how caring you are, my dear, and that's all that counts." Mama Mouse nuzzled him once more.

Seeing how lovingly Mama and Papa Mouse treated each other made the children feel better. They began to laugh again and tell stories.

Suddenly, Emmie broke loose from the others and ran to her uncle. She had an important question, which had just come to her, and she sincerely hoped Papa Mouse would agree to what she was about to ask him.

"Why is she running away from us?" Millie asked.

"Is she going to tattle?" Morris was a little worried. "I didn't mean to kick her. It was an accident. And it wasn't hard at all. Just a little bump."

"Don't be silly," Mollie chided her brother. "She probably thought it was a love bump. I saw her smile. I believe she likes you. She has even told me that she finds your short tail cute, and she would like to nibble a piece of your good ear off to make both even."

"Now you are teasing me for sure," Morris said. Of course, he wouldn't want his sister to know that he felt flattered.

In the meantime, little Emmie had reached Papa Mouse and tried to get his attention. When he finally looked at her and asked what she wanted, she blurted out, "Uncle, will you take me along when you go to my parents? I promise I will take quick enough steps to keep up with you. Didn't you notice how fast I could go when we came here? Please, please, take me along."

Papa Mouse crinkled his forehead. That's how hard he had to think. Then he said, "Emmie, dear, I would like to have the company, but …"

Mama Mouse finished the sentence for him. "But you should stay here so you can practice with us. Also, the long walk might exhaust you so much that, when you come back, you will not be strong enough to sing with us. Now, that would be a shame. All this hard work for nothing. I say you should stay right here. After the concert, you can go home with your parents. We will miss you, though."

Very disappointed and with her head hanging low, little Emmie returned to her cousins.

"They won't let me go along." She whimpered.

"Go where?" the cousins asked in unison.

"To my parents. I asked if I could accompany your father when he goes to talk to my mom and dad. He's not going to take me." Now Emmie's tears really began to flow. "And your mother also said I should stay here. She made all kinds of excuses."

"It's probably for the best. Honestly. Sometimes our parents know what is best for us. Now stop crying, Emmie. We love you." For good measure, Mollie gave her cousin a light cheek swipe.

As soon as they all returned home, they searched the kitchen for food and found plenty. Then, after a short rest, Papa Mouse announced that he would be on his way to the next town, and he would try hard to return as quickly as possible.

"Wish your father the best of luck, children," Mama Mouse said. "He will be off on a mission of great importance."

A moment later she added, "I'm glad he has a clear night to travel. Did you, by any chance, look at the beautiful stars in the sky? One was much bigger and brighter than the others, and I could swear it was blinking at me. I believe it was a good omen that all will go well."

"I wonder …" Mollie said.

"Wonder what?" Papa Mouse asked.

"I wonder if this could be the star of Bethlehem, only this time it will lead our papa to the next town."

"Perhaps, dear child," Papa Mouse said and smiled.

Papa Mouse Did Well

The day of the final rehearsal arrived. All week long, Mollie had been nervous. She was afraid her choir members might forget to practice, not remember the melody, perhaps even completely forget to show up for that last singing before the actual performance.

Mama Mouse had her own worries. What if the singers had not told their friends and neighbors about the show? An audience would be nice, a real big audience. And did they remember the food for after the show? At least one worry was gone. Her husband had just safely returned from his trip, and he had immediately assured her that he had

145

done his part as best as he possibly could. Unfortunately, he could only bring his brother-in-law with him. His sister preferred to stay home with her children. The boys, supposedly, had refused to walk the distance. Hear their sister sing? "Foolish nonsense," they had said.

When Emmie got a glimpse of her father, right after he had come through the hole, she was overjoyed. She acted as if she had not seen him in years. "Oh, Papa, you have come!" she cried.

"Did you think I would miss seeing my Emmie in the great performance? I've told all my friends about it, and, yes, some are going to come. They want to hear with their own ears what I've been bragging about. And … I guess you will be proud of me when I show you – and everybody here – what I've brought with me."

"What did you bring, Papa? Will you show us?"

"But of course. Just wait a minute, and I will bring it all in. It's heavy. Your uncle had to help me carry it. One had to have it on his back while the other held it in place. We took turns."

At once, Mollie, Millie and Morris came running to welcome their uncle. Their father, too, of course. All wanted to see what the two early-morning arrivals had brought with them. They could not see the items right away, because they were rolled up in pieces of old newspaper.

"Who wants to help?" Papa Mouse asked.

"Let me! Let me!" they all shouted together.

"Let Emmie help," the uncle decided, "because the things are from her own hometown."

And so Emmie tugged here and tugged there until the contents was revealed.

"This smells good!" she shouted immediately. "I see a big chunk of cheese. And cake. And bread. And … what is this? Isn't it what is called tunsel?"

"Not tunsel, Emmie." Mama Mouse corrected her niece. "It is called tinsel."

"Oh, yes, now I remember. That's what we decorated ourselves with when we went to that one rehearsal. Some mice laughed at us, and others thought it was beautiful. Are we now going to decorate our place with it?"

"No, Mollie," Papa Mouse said. "We will give a strand to every singer to put on the head. Mr. Rat, I'm sure, will wear his hat, and we mice wear tinsel. It will look festive."

Uncle nodded. He was glad he had been able to snitch that supply of the glittery stuff from the floor, where the careless people of his home had left it after decorating a tree in their living room.

"Great idea!" Mollie was delighted. Then she turned to her mother and asked, "Don't you think so, Mama?"

"I certainly do." With a big smile, she went to the two present-bearers and thanked them.

The youngsters, encouraging the adults to join their foursome, began to dance while merrily singing, "Tomorrow, tomorrow, we'll have a wonderful time tomorrow." It was a joyful celebration.

Final Rehearsal

"Shall we take the glittery stuff – the tinsel I mean – with us and distribute it to the singers?" Uncle Mouse asked.

"No way!" Mama Mouse protested. "They might lose it or forget to bring it tomorrow. The young ones may even play with it and shred it to pieces."

Uncle Mouse nodded and said, "You are right. The stuff is valuable, and we cannot replace it."

"What about the food?" Papa Mouse wanted to know. "Should we store it in the woodshed until tomorrow?"

"Have you lost your wits, dear?" Mama Mouse shook her head in total disbelief. "Do you honestly think it would still be there tomorrow when we need it?" Then she shook her head some more and said, "You men come up with the craziest ideas. Is it, perhaps, that you didn't get enough sleep? Now your brains are all fuzzy."

"What is going on here?" Mollie, having heard the loud word exchange, came closer to find out the reason for the noise.

Mama Mouse turned to her and said, "It's nothing important. The two here had some silly ideas, and I gave them my opinion." She pointed to Papa and Uncle Mouse, who sheepishly looked away.

"Oh!" Mollie gave a sigh of relief. "But isn't it about time to leave? Morris, Millie and Emmie can hardly wait. They are so excited. And I am, too."

"Okay, tell them we are ready." Mama Mouse gave her husband a little push, for, as was customary, he should be first through the hole. She stayed back until all others were safely out.

As usual, they proceeded with the utmost caution.

"Quickly, quickly!" Papa Mouse suddenly shouted. "I hear tiny footsteps that must belong to a people toddler. Where there is a small people child, a grownup is not far behind."

Seconds later, a big thud could be heard. This was followed by a scream. Then a constant crying.

Papa Mouse dared to stop in his tracks to stare in the direction of the source of that crying. What did he see? At the bottom of the stairs lay the screaming people child, and racing down the steps was a woman, no doubt the mother of the fallen one.

"Come! Run! Out through our secret exit!" he ordered the rest of his family. "This people mother will pay no attention to us now. She has to look after her child."

So … seven mice made it out of the building without being detected. They safely crossed the parking lot and gave sighs of relief when on the field.

A light snow was beginning to fall, and Morris had fun trying to catch flakes on his tongue. Emmie imitated him for a few moments, but then she gave up.

"Don't inhale too much of that frigid air, Morris," Mama Mouse warned. "It may ruin your voice."

Morris thought this was the silliest remark. While catching snowflakes, his mouth was not really open to let air in, because his tongue sealed the opening. *Sometimes, Mama is overly cautious,* he thought, but he did not resume the fun until his mother had turned around again and her back was turned to him.

The girls giggled, and as soon as the snow was coming down harder, they, too, took up Morris's game. It made walking across the wintery field more interesting.

Mr. Rat awaited them at the entrance to the woodshed. He was glad when the church mouse family came into sight. "I am so very relieved to see you all," he greeted them a moment later.

"Why?" Papa Mouse asked. "Didn't you think we would come? This is a very important rehearsal. We have to be here."

"But, you know, things can always come in the way. Unexpected things."

"I honestly don't know what brings that to your mind. You confuse me, Mr. Rat."

"Well, you see …"

"See what?"

"I noticed the big commotion at the church where you live. Sirens blaring. Lights flashing … from a big vehicle. It was not the red one with the ladder that comes when there's a fire, but it was the other big one. So I feared that, with all the commotion going on and so many people running around, it was not safe for you to come out without being discovered."

"I guess we made it out just in time. We missed that great commotion. But I have an idea what it was all about."

"What do you think caused it? Please, tell."

"As we were all slipping out of our place, a people youngster fell down the stairs. The child must have been hurt badly. People do that. When something hurts them or is broken, they call for help. We mice suffer in silence. You rats do the same."

"So true." Mr. Rat nodded.

"You two fellows are having quite a conversation," Mama Mouse interrupted. "But don't you think we better go in now? The others are waiting."

Indeed, they were. They seemed to be getting impatient already.

"Okay, okay, we are here. Let's get started!" Mama Mouse called out in a loud voice. And I see we already have Mollie's podium in place. Wonderful. Take your places, please."

It was a scramble, eager mice bumping into each other, trying to get to their assigned spots. The rats, since there were only a few of them, had it easier. Their only worry was not to miss the cue for beginning to play. But Mr. Rat was a good conductor, and they also knew not only to pay attention to him but to Mollie, too. Mainly to Mollie. Mr. Rat also took his cues from her. Since they were all smart rats – rats are usually smart, they could handle it. They were filled with confidence and found it unnecessary to get a last minute pep talk from Mr. Rat.

Mama Mouse was about to give Mr. Rat the sign to let his musicians know to pick up their instruments and begin the trumpet fanfare, when she noticed the rat director vigorously nodding to his orchestra members. Instead of picking up their instruments, they fumbled on the ground. Each lifted up something colorful. Party hats similar to Mr. Rat's! Soon, each rat wore one, and this made the amazed singers slightly envious.

"If we could all wear hats, it would be … very nice," one mouse said.

"I want one of those!" wide-eyed Priscilla shouted.

Of course, her mother shushed her and whispered something into the girl's ear, which, by the looks of it, did not make Priscilla happy.

"Wait until tomorrow," Mama Mouse said, "and then you will see the surprise we have for you. For all of you. And now, really, let's get started. Mr. Rat, are you ready? Mollie, all set?"

Yes, everybody was ready.

Big, impressive trumpet fanfare. A powerful drumroll. Then the singers and the rest of the musicians. Not a single mistake. On the first try. It was like a miracle.

Applause came from the back of the woodshed. Then there were shouts of appreciation. "Bravo, bravo, bravo!" Old Mrs. Moss and her companion had been sitting there, unnoticed throughout the rehearsal. Now the two came forward to thank the singers and instrumentalists for their wonderful performance.

"If you do so well tomorrow, I … I … wouldn't be surprised …" old Mrs. Moss halted to find the right words.

"What would not surprise you, Mrs. Moss?" Mollie asked.

"If not every mouse would want to learn how to sing."

Mollie laughed and bid farewell to Mrs. Moss and her companion. "See you tomorrow!" she called after them as they slowly made their way out of the woodshed.

"Wouldn't miss it!" Mrs. Moss called back.

Show Time!

"Please, let everything go well. Please, let everything go well." Mollie's plea sounded like a chant.

Mama Mouse heard it. She had been busy getting all the food together for the after-show reception and had her own worries. Listening to Mollie did not help her dilemma. "How are we supposed to transport this stuff?" she asked herself. Finally, she said it out loud enough to reach her husband's ears.

"I don't understand you females," he said. "One frets so much over the outcome of tonight's performance, and the other one cannot figure out how to get the food there. How did my sister's husband and I bring so much stuff here? Don't you remember? We packed it all up and carried it on our backs. That's how we will do it again."

Uncle Mouse stood by and laughed. "Helpless women," he mumbled. Then he dragged the package material out of the corner, for there it had been stored, and ordered, "Now hand me hard items first. Stale bread crusts. Those assorted cereals. Now the pieces of cookies. And the cheese scraps. Chunks of cake go on top. Is this all? Good. Emmie, hold the packaging. This way! I don't want it to slip down. Morris, come here. You have to help me tie this up. Good job."

"Why didn't I think of this?" Mama Mouse chided herself. "Perhaps it is a man's job."

Papa Mouse gave his wife a loving pat. Then he whispered into her ear, "We men, after all, have to be good for something."

"Oh, you," Mama Mouse whispered back and gave him an unexpected big pat.

"And how do we get all the tinsel there?" Mollie wanted to know.

"That's what you youngsters have to worry about. It shouldn't be so hard." Uncle Mouse looked at the children and then added, with a big grin, "You are always so smart about everything else."

"I know," Mollie said. "We divide the big glittery bundle into four parts, and then we all get to carry some."

"Good idea," Mama Mouse said. "But what is left for me?"

Papa Mouse laughed. "You carry the good wishes that all goes well. Then it will be a big load off Mollie's shoulders. She has carried it too long already. I've heard her incantations."

"Papa, you speak weird." Minnie made a face as if she had just bitten into a piece of sour lemon. "What does incan… whatever you said, mean?"

"I believe that's what they use when someone is singing a magic spell. Mollie kept chanting 'Please, let everything go well' over and over again as if she was trying to cast a spell on tonight's performance. A good spell, of course."

"My goodness, Uncle Mouse," Mollie exclaimed, "is this what it sounded like?"

"To me, yes." Uncle Mouse let out a hearty laugh. "Don't worry, dear Mollie, maybe your incantations work well."

It took a while until the silly remarks, back and forth, stopped, and then Mama Mouse advised everyone to better take a short nap before it was time to leave for the woodshed. Rested performers, she was sure, would be able to give a better show.

All too soon, she had to arouse them again. But after an initial drowsiness, they were eager to be on their way. Uncle Mouse carried the bag with food on his back, Papa Mouse held it in place, the children proudly carried the tinsel, and Mama Mouse, making up the rear of their strange parade, watched that nothing got dropped and left behind.

It was a beautiful evening. The stars above twinkled as if to wish them good luck. One star was exceptionally bright again, and Mollie imagined that this one probably looked very much like the star of Bethlehem. She wished she could have seen that tiny baby whose birthday was being celebrated by the people right about now. *I can try to imagine it while singing*, she thought. *I will sing for that baby boy.*

So, with something akin to love in her heart, Mollie entered the woodshed. She was determined to let this love shine so brightly that it would overflow into the hearts of her fellow singers and make them sing so beautiful that the precious baby would smile on them in delight. Somehow, it seemed as if her imagination had become reality.

More words she had heard the man in the white robe say came to mind, but what did they mean? Holy night. Peace on earth. Oh, there was so much more. If she could only remember.

Mollie was brought out of her thoughts by the din in the woodshed. Lots of spectators had already arrived. Many made it clear that curiosity had brought them there, and also the fun of sharing a meal after the show was over. They bragged about the food they had brought and how much they hoped others had been as generous.

"I'll be glad to get rid of the load on my back," Uncle Mouse said. "Someone please help me get it off."

This job fell on Papa Mouse, of course. Mama Mouse and the children had already moved to where the rat musicians and the mice singers were congregating. Her family needed to distribute the tinsel.

"I promised we would bring you something for the show," Mama Mouse said to the admiring crowd. "We will all wear glittering strands of tinsel. Now, what do you think of this?"

Such delight! The mice went crazy over the sight, and they could hardly wait to have their oh-so-beautiful, shiny strands of tinsel draped around their necks. The males wore their decorations as proudly as the females.

Mama Mouse, inspecting the group, suddenly shook her head. Then she said, "It doesn't look quite right to me. I think the boys and men look splendid with the tinsel around their necks, but the girls and the women … I believe they would benefit from wearing the tinsel on top of their heads … in a circle. Let me show you."

Then her eyes searched to the right, then to the left, and, finally, she called out loud, "Mollie, where are you? I need you to be the model!"

"But Mama, why are you shouting? I'm right here." Mollie had been standing behind her mother. Because Mama Mouse had failed to turn around, she had not seen her.

A giggling, started by Priscilla, rippled through the crowd. Moments later, Mama Mouse saw it fit to join in. But then she began her demonstration. She took the tinsel off her daughter's neck and arranged it on her head, in a perfect circle.

"Doesn't this look pretty?" she asked.

"Yes!" In chorus, the mice answered and immediately assisted each other in rearranging the glitter strands.

"Girls, girls, hurry up!" Papa Mouse sounded impatient. "The audience is getting restless."

"We're coming," the female mice answered and scurried to their places.

Wow, how impressive the group of performers looked! The rats with hats and the mice with sparkling tinsel. This warranted a round of applause.

"Remember, we are announcing an important event," Mollie reminded the group. "Trumpet and drum, let it be heard. Singers, be joyful, but remember the important part in which you admire the sleeping babe. You don't want to wake the little boy. Sing softly. Bells and xylophone, you know what to do. And at the end, we all get louder, because we want to announce to the world what we have seen. And now, group, let's vow the audience!"

Indeed, they did. Everything went exactly as Mollie had envisioned it. The voices blended. The orchestra members came in at the correct times and played with gusto when required and softly when it was called for. If there was, by chance, anybody in the audience who did not understand the meaning of the musical story, it was not the performers' fault, because they sang with all the emotion needed to paint the picture.

It seemed as if the applause would never stop.

But then – oh no! – could it be? Was great danger awaiting them outdoors, even in their midst?

Unbeknownst to the performers and mice in the audience, an owl had been hiding in the rafters. When, suddenly, it flew circles above them, they feared for their lives. But the owl called down to them, "Do not be afraid. I will not harm you. I heard you practice for many days, and I was enchanted. I simply had to come and listen to you perform. I loved your show. Thank you for letting me listen, and peace be with you." Then it fluttered out of the woodshed.

From outside, near the entrance, came a chorus of meows. Three cats had been sitting there during the entire performance, listening to the music. They, too, thanked the mice and the rats for the great pleasure, and then they wished them a merry Christmas.

"We will go back home now, where it is warm," a calico cat said. "You keep on celebrating. Honestly, no harm will come to you."

And then, before running off, those three cats meowed something that sounded like thanks and goodbyes and happy holiday wishes.

Another well-wisher was outside, hidden in a tall tree. It was the hawk that had also listened to the concert. "Merry Christmas and peace be with you," the big bird's call came from above. "Your music sounded heavenly. Thank you for letting me hear it." Having said this, the hawk left its lofty perch and flew into the starry night.

Mice and rats were relieved when the intruders were gone, but they could hardly believe that they had all left in peace.

What is this magic of Christmas? Mollie thought. *Peace on earth. That's what the people man in the white robe had talked about for weeks. Wouldn't it be wonderful, if such peace could last forever?*

"Are you dreaming again?" Mama Mouse asked. "Let's go and eat. There is so much food to enjoy. A celebration is in order."

PEACE on EARTH

Encore

The concert in the woodshed had been a great success. It would not have been so had Mr. Rat not brought his talented friends with their instruments to accompany the singers. The mice knew it, and they were grateful. How could they thank the rats?

Upon Mama Mouse's urging, Papa Mouse took Mr. Rat aside and said," We cannot part without congratulating each other for tonight's success. We worked hard together, as friends. We could not have done it separately. What can we mice do to show our appreciation?"

"I know. I have a brilliant idea. I think it is a super idea."

"What is it? Please, tell me, Mr. Rat."

"If your singers would be willing …"

"Just come out with it. Say it!"

"… willing to come to the dump tomorrow evening to give an encore. I am sure all the rats would love to hear the concert. My instrumentalists are so wound up they are more than eager to do the Christmas number again."

"Mr. Rat, you just had the best idea. Wait here, I have to quickly tell the singers about this wonderful plan before they all disappear for home. I will be back in a second."

And so, without consulting Mama Mouse and Mollie and the others of his family, Papa Mouse stormed over to the singers who were still enjoying the after-show feast.

"Listen, all of you, we have one more engagement. Tomorrow evening. At the dump. A performance for the rats. Are you coming?"

"Yes, yes, we will be there!"

How was that concert? Fabulous. And the friendship between mice and rats thickened. And it was all due to Mollie's Christmas choir.

And guess what? The cat, the owl, and the hawk were there to listen again. They had come in peace.

Ah, the wonder of Christmas!

Merry
Christmas
to
all !!!

Mollie Mouse and Her Christmas Choir

CPSIA information can be obtained
at www.ICGtesting.com
Printed in the USA
LVHW011502281019
635545LV00002B/573